THE
PREMIER'S
DAUGHTER

JEREMY AKERMAN

The Premier's Daughter
© 2023 Jeremy Akerman

Cover image by the author
Cover design: Rebekah Wetmore
Editor: Andrew Wetmore

ISBN: 978-1-990187-76-6
First edition May 2023

MOOSE HOUSE
PUBLICATIONS

2475 Perotte Road
Annapolis County, NS
B0S 1A0

moosehousepress.com
info@moosehousepress.com

We live and work in Mi'kma'ki, the ancestral and unceded territory of the Mi'kmaw People. This territory is covered by the "Treaties of Peace and Friendship" which Mi'kmaw and Wolastoqiyik (Maliseet) People first signed with the British Crown in 1725. The treaties did not deal with surrender of lands and resources but in fact recognized Mi'kmaq and Wolastoqiyik (Maliseet) title and established the rules for what was to be an ongoing relationship between nations. We are all Treaty people.

Also by Jeremy Akerman

and available from Moose House Publications

Memoir
Outsider

Politics
What Have You Done for Me Lately? – revised edition

Fiction
Black Around the Eyes – revised edition
The Affair at Lime Hill
In Search of Dr. Dee (coming in 2023)

This book is dedicated to the Class of 1970 of the
Nova Scotia Legislature,
of which I was honoured to be a member.

In memory of:

Roger Bacon
Frank Bezanson
Garnet Brown
John Buchanan
John Burke
Joe Casey
Benoit Comeau
Jim Connolly
Walton Cook
Mike Delory
Gerald Doucet
Ralph Fiske
Bill Gillis
George Henley
Harry How
Fisher Hudson
Harold Huskilson
Ken Jones
Mike Laffin
Bob Lindsay
Loyd MacDonald

Paul MacEwan
John Archie MacKenzie
Tom MacKeough
Jim MacLean
Scott MacNutt
George Mitchell
Fraser Mooney
Peter Nicholson
Leonard Pace
Gerald Regan
George Riley
Gerald Ritcey
Gerald Sheehey
Ike Smith
Raymond Smith
George Snow
Allan Sullivan
Victor Thorpe
Harvey Veinot
Ron Wallace
Maurice Zinck

And in honour of the Survivors:

Glen Bagnell
Jack Hawkins

Angus MacIsaac
Gordon Tidman

And to all Members of the Nova Scotia Legislature, living or dead.

The Premier's Daughter

1

To have said that spring was in the air would have been misleading. It was still April, but one of those unusual but joyful, meteorological occurrences had brought a sudden preview of summer, with twenty-four-degree temperatures and blazing blue skies.

Residents of Halifax had seen similarly strange twists in the weather before, and knew it would not last. They knew it would be at least another month and a half before they could rely on continuous warm days and nights, but they would make the most of this God sent phenomenon and gladly, if temporarily, throw off their sweaters and topcoats and take to the streets in shorts and summer dresses.

The unseasonable heat, however, while welcome to most, was not conducive to either comfort or friendly relations at the Nova Scotia Legislature. Here, the Members, in business suits and buttoned-up shirts and blouses, squirmed in a space which was built to accommodate the representatives elected by the voters more than two hundred years before.

When the Assembly met for the first time here in 1819, it must be supposed that they had the good sense not to meet in hot weather; although, since a proper heating system was not installed until 1889, they must have greatly suffered if they met during the winter months.

Since they first convened in 1758, the Members had moved from pillar to post around the city, often meeting in private houses, until, in 1811, they passed *An Act for erecting a Province House, on the Ground where the old Government House now stands for the meeting of the different Branches of the Legislature and other public purposes.*

The Act stipulated that the building was to follow a design produced by one John Merrick, whose selection, whether for reasons of patronage or availability, was somewhat curious. He was a painter, not an architect at all.

In any event, though they spent 52,000 pounds on its construction, and lavished on it ironwork brought all the way from Scotland, the entire building was only just over 40 metres long and 20 metres wide. Since the building had to contain a law court and two chambers, of necessity the meeting place for the Members of the Lower House was relatively small, albeit with a high ceiling.

An image dated 1879 shows there were thirty-two Members at that time, and although various alterations were made over the intervening years, today's fifty-five elected Members are required to sit in essentially the same space. Visitors to the chamber exclaim with delight that, unlike the grandiose and lofty legislatures of Ontario, Quebec and the western provinces, Nova Scotia's is "intimate" and "cozy"; but for those who work there it can be crowded, if not cramped.

Such circumstances are not always propitious for calm tempers or feelings of brotherly love.

Thus it was that on a beautiful day like this one, many Members of the Legislature wished they could be elsewhere, preferably in the Botanical Gardens or Point Pleasant Park, especially since they were now engaged in the often tedious exercise known as "Estimates." In these sessions, with The Speaker gone from the Chair, various ministers of the Crown sought approval for the monies their departments believed they would need to carry out their responsibilities.

This presented opportunities for the Opposition to "grill" ministers at some length, and if a minister became testy or evasive his or her ordeal would certainly be amplified. And unless the Estimates were of a department which was uncontroversial or presented by a popular minister who was collaborative and harmonious, they could drag on in a stupefying if not somniferous fashion.

This was the case with old Ernest Maddingly, the Deputy Premier, who was a gentleman of the old school, obliging and, unless in exceptional circumstances, not unduly partisan. The constituents of his remote, rural constituency had been sending him back to the House for almost forty years and now, in his late seventies, he was widely thought to be in his last term in the Assembly.

His position of Deputy Premier as second in command to Premier Brenton Granger was purely nominal, only intended to give a nod of recognition to his years of service, as Granger was not a man given to encouraging anyone, even temporarily, to poach on his preserves, still less to get any ideas about taking his job. In addition, Maddingly was Provincial Secretary, the minister responsible for a grab bag of miscellaneous responsibilities such as registrations and writs, formal documents, and licences, all generally regarded as the least interesting and non contentious matters.

At one time, the Provincial Secretary was the most important official in the province, but that time was long gone. As Maddingly droned on, only one Member was encouraging him by asking questions, while several members were asleep and others were lazily tapping on their laptops, or looking longingly out of the windows.

Sitting on the Government front bench were Granger's cabinet, pretending to be enthralled by Maddingly's presentation. Prominent among them were Stephanie Gilmour, Minister of Social Services, a good-looking woman in her mid-forties; and Wendell Proctor, Minister of Labour, a very tall, handsome black man of thirty-nine.

Sitting immediately behind them was the Chief Whip, Tom Aldridge, a good-looking, athletic man in his mid-forties. Behind him, on the back benches, looking perpetually outraged, was Zandili Joseph, a very large black woman who moved in her seat as if it gave her continuing offence.

Up in the front row of the Speaker's gallery, an old man leaned over the rail, listening intently, his eyes darting this way and that, not missing any movement, however slight, on the floor. This was Arthur Cramp, the party chairman who, at eighty-two, had seen the party through good times and bad, all the while acting as its prime mover, shaker and, when necessary, its fixer of slips, scandals, crimes and misdemeanours.

Cramp and Granger were as close as peas in a pod, the Premier seldom acting on any matter without first consulting "Uncle Arthur". While, for the most part Cramp was a forgiving man, understanding of human foibles and weaknesses, it was an extremely unwise MLA, wishing for advancement within the party or government, who offended Uncle Arthur.

The Granger government was coming to the end of its second term. It had done well by all accounts, had few scandals, personal or administrative, had managed to balance the books, and had won the last election in a landslide. Now, with the polls looking favourable, Brenton Granger was generally expected to win a third term in office.

Granger was a big, bluff man in his late fifties, with an adoring wife, Florence, a son and three daughters, two of them twins, all of whom had been blessed with astonishingly good looks. He was a church-goer, a former university football star, a veteran, a remarkable public speaker, and a man to whom people could easily relate. He was a steady, level-headed man, and what he lacked in brilliance and imagination he more than compensated for in common sense.

Much of Granger's appeal with the voters had to do with his apparently family-oriented, upright and clean-living nature. What all but a very few people did not know was that Granger was carrying a secret, one of some years standing, but which now was threatening to bring his world down about his ears in dramatic fashion.

2

The sun's heat was just starting to weaken and it cast long, gently waving shadows from the trees planted in the sidewalks of residential streets in the provincial capital. Except for the fact that many of the trees had only a few leaves or none yet, it really was like summer, something evidenced by the large numbers of people who were scantily dressed.

But night would draw in rapidly, and soon the cold would return, likely for many more weeks to come. The evening rush hour had ended, so the traffic was fairly light, and fewer than a dozen people plied their way from their workplaces. Others were out walking their dogs, both pets and owners grateful for this short respite from the harsher weather.

With a graceful, lilting walk, Heidi Granger approached the bus stop, joining three others in the queue. One was apparently a domestic worker of some kind, possibly making her way to her home in a less salubrious part of the city; the man seemed to be bakery worker whose coveralls bore remains of flour; and the third was a very old woman whom the unusually clement weather had caused to forget to wear any socks or stockings.

Heidi thought she could see the disappointments of their lives in their faces, and resolved, though she did not know quite how, not to end up like them. With her lack of experience she imagined it could be achieved by positive thinking, although she acknowledged to herself that coming from a privileged background might have something to do with having a buoyant outlook on life. Having been the premier's daughter for almost eight years of her life certainly had its advantages.

Heidi may have been relatively inexperienced, but she certainly did not look it. In her manner, she appeared to be much older than her twenty-four years, carrying herself with a cool-headed confidence, and considerable class.

Naturally, it helped that she was extremely attractive, being of slightly taller than average height, with shiny, bouncy blonde hair into which she had pushed her sunglasses, large, laughing blue eyes and an alluring figure. Taking advantage of the weather, she was wearing red shorts, a white T-shirt and sneakers, and carried a shiny, red bag on a long strap, over which she had draped a white sweater.

The older lady seemed not to notice her presence, and the domestic gave Heidi only the most cursory of glances; but the man, his eyes crowded with memories, regrets and longing, stared at what to him was an angelic face.

Her happy, wondering eyes caught his gaze, and he quickly looked away when she gave him a wide, innocent smile.

At length, the bus arrived and they boarded, Heidi's step lighter, more hopeful than the others. As the bus pulled away, a small dog strained at its leash, barking at the wheels as its owner hauled it back out of the way.

The man carefully sneaked another glance at Heidi, thinking ruefully of the contrast between her and the woman who was waiting at home for him. The domestic eyed her with a mixture of disdain and jealousy, thinking that nobody deserved to be both young and beautiful, because she, to her eternal regret, had never been either.

On the short journey across the city, while the others gazed vacantly out of the windows, Heidi read from a copy of Jean Anouilh's play *The Rehearsal*, so she did not notice two large signs in front of a recently built, brick Fundamentalist meeting house. In heavy, censorious, black letters the first announced:

THE WAGES OF SIN IS DEATH—Romans 6:24

The second sign exhorted the misspelled belief that

LOVE ENURETH ALL THINGS—I Corinthians 13:7

The bus stopped across the road from an imposing old church, the sign in front of which indicated it was dedicated to Saint Michael the Archangel.

As she alighted, Heidi recalled that St. Michael was considered a champion of justice who was usually depicted slaying a dragon with a large sword, while waving a banner above his head and holding a pair of scales. Not easy, thought Heidi, to deal with a ferocious beast while brandishing the accoutrements of the righteous.

St. Michael's was an old, grey, stone church, built well over a hundred years previously, with tall stained glass windows. All rather noble, considered Heidi, and guaranteed to make you feel guilty even if you had done nothing wrong.

She had to walk down the street a little before she came to the church hall, clearly a poor relation of the parent since it was built of wood with concrete foundations and had been tacked on to the main building at a later, less prosperous or less religious date.

The sign outside announced the reason for Heidi's visit:

St. Michael's Players
Jean Anouilh's THE REHEARSAL
"Auditions" tonight, starting 7pm
Tom Aldridge, Director.

Heidi paused to wonder why the sign maker had placed the word auditions in quotation marks. Was it out of punctuational ignorance, or because the person thought that only so-called, as opposed to real, auditions would take place here tonight? There was no way of knowing, or why only yesterday she had seen in a restaurant window a sign for Fish and "Chips".

So, Tom Aldridge was directing this production, which was interesting because Heidi knew him slightly from her father's political meetings, he being one of the premier's supporters in the Legislature. She had never spoken to Aldridge, having only seen him from a distance, at which times he had struck her as a kindly man and quite handsome, though much older than her. She wondered how much older, guessing that Aldridge was at least twenty years her senior, maybe more.

There was a line of people outside the door, all of them having copies of the play in hand and earnestly studying its contents. One intense young man with a wispy beard and knees protruding from his jeans, was muttering to himself with his eyes closed. Clearly, she thought, he had memorized the lines for his audition piece and was, in the vernacular, "getting into character."

Heidi joined the line-up and, as she waited, from the open door, she heard the voice of a hopeful, male auditionee carry in the warm air:

The prince desires Sylvia—perhaps he loves her too.
Why should the prince be refused the right to love so deeply?
The whole court will conspire to destroy the loves of Harlequin
    and Sylvia.
In short, it is the story of an elegant and sophisticated crime.

3

When it was finally Heidi's turn to audition, a woman called Marge, who said she was the assistant stage manager, called her inside. Heidi followed her into the large, barn-like space which had been converted into a theatre by erecting a small stage at one end, installing rows of raked seating and hanging strategically placed lighting bars.

They passed two would-be actors who were on their way out. By the looks on their faces, their auditions had not been successful.

Marge conducted Heidi to the stage and asked her to climb up on to it.

When she looked out, she saw Tom Aldridge, who was dressed in jeans with a denim shirt and a loose, navy cardigan. Aldridge introduced himself and a large, unkempt woman clothed entirely in violent purple, whom he announced was Phemie Gallant, the stage manager.

Together with Marge, who now appeared to be going to sleep, they sat at several card tables which had been pushed together. The tables were littered with sheets of paper, scripts and, Heidi noticed, a list of names, most of which had been crossed out with a black marker. These, she guessed, were those who had already auditioned, had been found wanting and were summarily rejected.

Aldridge was obviously a doodler, as Heidi could see pages of scribbles and drawings in front of him. He was stretched out in a cheap wooden chair, almost horizontal with his feet on the table, while Phemie busied herself making notes, apparently about Heidi's appearance.

At the very back of the hall, languidly leaning against a pillar and casting a benevolent eye over the proceedings, was a man wearing a clerical collar. This, she assumed, must be Father Jeffery Milton, the parish priest, about whom she had heard some gossip, but could not remember what it was.

At one side was a man in his forties, apparently also waiting to be auditioned.

Phemie asked Heidi's name, age, address and telephone number, whether she had done any theatre before, and if so what she had performed and where. Heidi dutifully answered all these questions, noticing as she did so that Aldridge was now sitting bolt upright and looking straight at her.

Heidi walked over to the side of the stage and deposited her bag, sweater and script. When she walked back to centre stage, she noticed that Aldridge was now standing up, holding her in an intense stare, which made her wonder if she had made a mistake by defying some obscure theatrical convention.

"Leonard," said Aldridge, calling to the man, "will you go up, please? Leonard will be reading with you, Heidi. Is that alright?"

"Sure."

"Good. Don't be nervous."

"I'm not nervous," said Heidi.

Aldridge seemed to be flustered by her reply. "Good, good," he said. "A lot of people are nervous when they audition. I just wanted to make sure you're not."

"No, not a bit," Heidi replied, hoping her confidence would not be interpreted as impudence.

"Then you're a very unusual woman," said Aldridge. He paused, still gazing at her, then said, "Okay, let's do it."

Heidi and Leonard took up their positions and did their scene. It was only a short scene, but Aldridge had them do it many times.

> Leonard: *I'll never know then, even by hearsay, how love is set in motion.*
> Heidi: *I could never bear anyone to touch me. Yet when he took me in his arms, I felt I had come to the end of my journey. I had something of my own at last.*

"Beautiful!" Aldridge said. "Wonderful. Thank you so much."

Phemie, whose intuition told her something out of the ordinary was happening, leaned across to Marge. "Why do I have a feeling that one is already cast?"

Marge raised an eyebrow at her, then called out to Heidi, "Thank you, we'll let you know. We'll be in touch."

Heidi gathered up her possessions, climbed down from the stage and headed for the door.

"Give me a minute," said Aldridge to Phemie. "Don't call the next one just yet."

He followed Heidi out of the hall, catching up with her in the churchyard. "Excuse me," he called.

As he later told his friend Wendell, when she turned around his heart almost stopped beating.

"Yes?"

"Are you who I think you are?" asked Aldridge.

"Who do you think I am?"

"Are you my boss's daughter?"

"That depends upon who your boss is," replied Heidi, enjoying the game.

"Are you Brenton Granger's girl?"

"He has three girls, but, yes, Brenton Granger is my dad."

"Ah. Have I seen you before?"

Several of the people in the lineup were now looking curiously at them; some were close enough to overhear what they were saying.

"I don't know who you've seen, but I've seen you once or twice at party meetings."

"That would explain it."

"Explain what?"

"Explain why I had a feeling about you."

"What kind of feeling?"

At this Aldridge fell into a state of confusion, and turned back towards the hall. "I must go. Others to audition," he said, clearly unsettled. "Nice to have met you. I'll see you soon, when we get the production going."

"Does that mean I've got the part?"

"Oh yes," said Aldridge earnestly. "You've got the part."

4

Tom Aldridge's life had not been an easy one.

His mother, Gertie, was a "bay wop", a fisherman's daughter from Little Bay Islands, Newfoundland, who had known grinding poverty in her youth. Her family had left for St. John's many years before their neighbours were driven out by the federal Cod Moratorium in 1992. When, in 1954, the government of Joey Smallwood offered monetary assistance through the Centralization Programme to people who would move from the outports to larger centres, they took it.

The relocation subsidy was between $301 and $600 per family. By 1959, 29 communities containing around 2,400 people had been resettled with government assistance.

In St. John's they had known nobody and could find little work, so in desperation they moved to Cape Breton, where Gertie's father's widowed sister lived. Within two years, both parents were dead, apparently from extended nutritional anemia and edema caused by micronutrient deficiencies of vitamin A, iron and iodine.

Gertie's aunt told her that the doctors didn't know what they were talking about, and that her parents had died of broken hearts.

Gertie continued to live with her aunt until she met and married Murdoch, Tom's father.

Murdoch was a coal miner in Glace Bay, Cape Breton, until at age 40 he was disabled by pneumoconiosis, or black lung. After that he hung about the house day in and day out, drinking rum whenever he could get hold of it.

His mother had told Tom that his father was driving her to an early grave, and so it proved when she died at the age of 44, a year younger than her son's present age. His father soon followed her, having suffered a right ventricular failure apparently brought on by pulmonary insufficiency and alcoholism.

Tom worked at various jobs in the area, from cleaning toilets, to flipping burgers, to working in a bakery, to working at the ferry terminal in North Sydney. Eventually, he managed to get a student loan and went to St. Francis Xavier University in Antigonish, some two hundred kilometres away on the mainland. There he was a diligent, but not outstanding, student, studying Business Administration and staying for four years to get his BBA.

As is often the case in life, someone else's misfortune turned out to be his good fortune, because the year he graduated with his degree, the manager of the small, local credit union dropped dead.

Tom applied for the job, not dreaming he would be successful; but due to the paucity of even remotely qualified applicants, he was hired for a probationary period of six months. Never had he worked harder than in that half year, both at the job itself and in assiduously cultivating members of the board of the credit union by giving them plenty of attention and flattery.

It was while flattering the board chairman, Archie MacDonald , that he met Archie's daughter, Iris. Tom started going out with her on a regular basis.

Iris was a slight, not to say thin, but attractive woman, a little younger than himself, who was taken with Tom's good looks and "respectable" position in the community. Her father told her that, as a manager, Tom was "a good prospect" who, if he played his cards right, "had a job for life."

Since she was a child, Iris had had it drummed into her that "security" was the most important achievement of all, and that if one attained that, all other good things would follow. Tom, on the other hand, had frequently been told that to succeed one had to have a wife, and Archie had more than once hinted that his future tenure as manager of the credit union might depend upon it.

Whether either of them was even remotely in love was debatable, although everyone thought, and said, it was a perfect match and heartily congratulated them both. Besides which, Tom, asked himself, who knew what love really was, what were it distinguishing characteristics, and would one recognize them if they appeared?

For her part, Iris had been taught by her mother that love "came later", after the essential requirements of job, home, security, and children had been taken care of. So Iris convinced herself she was doing the right thing, that she would be content, if not actually happy, and that if this magical thing called love did transpire, it would be a pleasant and welcome bonus.

Archie and his wife, Annie Mae, gave them a splendid wedding, a real "show-off" affair with all the trimmings, something which must have cost them a small fortune. There were over 200 guests, hired cars, a three-course meal, a six-piece band and expensive favours for everyone.

It was said by most that Iris, in her costly white gown, looked satisfied, although a few said her look was rather complacent and self-approving.

Everyone said that Tom looked very charming and handsome in his tuxedo, but some asked if his demeanour showed not that he felt he was at the beginning of a journey, but at the end of it.

They moved into a renovated, former coal company official's house on Fraser Avenue, which Archie had furnished in rather too lavish a fashion. Tom was confirmed in his job at the credit union and Iris became a home maker. They were at ease, they were untroubled, they were comfortable and they had security.

Two years later, at Iris's urging, Tom applied for a position in a large credit union in one of the Halifax suburbs and was successful. Archie did not approve of their moving, but Annie Mae talked him round, pointing out that with the improved salary and greater social opportunities, their daughter would have a better life. So, with Archie's help, they bought a small house in their new community and settled in.

Shortly thereafter, Andrew was born and, while it would be an exaggeration to say that their cup ranneth over, they were as content as most people have any right to expect. The little lad was, as one would anticipate, the apple of his father's eye; but while she was never cruel to him, or ever deprived him of anything he wanted, Iris invariably acted as if the boy was something of an inconvenience.

This period of delicate equilibrium continued until Andrew was five when, on a very snowy, windy day, Iris slipped on black ice in the street and was run down by an enormous, skidding, Sobey's refrigerator truck. She was taken to hospital, where she clung to life for almost a day before giving up the ghost.

The attending physician, Dr. Rahman, told Tom that Iris had never had a chance of survival, having sustained many broken bones, blunt head trauma and serious spinal damage. The police told him that it was nobody's fault and had just been "one of those things."

Iris had one of the biggest funerals that St. Michael's had ever seen. Those who did not attend from love or liking for her, did so out of respect or friendship for Tom. The service was painful for all concerned, not least for little Andrew, because the aging priest, Father Geoffrey's predecessor, rambled on at great length, occasionally giving his listeners the impression he was eulogizing somebody entirely different from the deceased.

Many, the older women in particular, said that the sight of Tom standing hand in hand with Andrew at the top of the church steps was one of the most poignant and moving of their lives. This image of acute suffering and childish bewilderment was recorded for posterity by a photographer from the local newspaper, in whose pages it appeared two days later.

Unable to look after Andrew properly while attending to the affairs of the credit union, Tom reluctantly, begrudgingly, handed the child over to Annie Mae to raise, on the understanding that there would never, at any time, be a barrier to his seeing his son.

So, with this arrangement agreeable to all parties, including Andrew, who adored his grandmother, they continued their uneventful lives until another twist of fate intervened.

Dr. MacLeod, the constituency's long-serving MLA, died suddenly while on vacation in Florida, and the local executive approached Tom, asking if he would allow them to nominate him for the resultant by-election. Tom, whose life seemed largely pointless without his small family around him any more, agreed to their proposition.

He was opposed for the nomination but, as the constituency chairwoman, Annette Nearing, told him, his opponent was "only the village idiot," and Tom won handily.

During the ensuing by-election, Tom learned how much fun politics could be and that, even in foul weather, he enjoyed canvassing round the houses, where he generally received a warm and friendly reception. This, Annette explained to him, was due in part to his having become something of a sympathetic hero as a result of the famous newspaper photograph.

On Election Day, Tom received 4,500 votes to his nearest opponent's 3,800, with his other opponent getting only 1,900. Tom resigned from the credit union and became a full-time politician. Thereafter, Tom had carried the party's banner twice more, being re-elected with increasing majorities.

Until now, Tom Aldridge could not actually say he had ever known love, except for the love he bore for his son. Political life had certainly provided many opportunities for intimate encounters. It was amazing to Tom that the combination of being a Member of the Legislature and a single man would throw so many women his way. In his crude, down to earth, way Uncle Arthur Cramp described this phenomenon as the "celebrity fuck".

It was fun, all right, but none of the contacts were lasting, and few much more than entertainment. He had dated Stephanie Gilmour a number of times but, while it was clear she was greatly enamoured of him, he could not quite "see it to the starting gate", as Wendell put it.

The truth was that, while Stephanie was very attractive and he liked her enormously, she was too stylish, too rich, too opinionated and too high-minded for him. As he told Wendell, being with her sometimes made him feel as if he were spitting in church.

But today, he had met Heidi. Heidi! He thought of all the clichés he had read and heard about love—stunned by love, love at first sight, being bowled over, swept off his feet, bursting with joy, walking on air—and absolutely all of them applied to how he felt about Heidi. He was confused, disturbed, agitated, intoxicated, anxious, fearful, thrilled, uplifted, and extremely joyful.

That she was a good twenty years his junior, and was the premier's daughter, certainly posed what seemed like insuperable barriers to anything ever developing between them, but he knew he had to pursue it wherever it might lead. It was not as if he had a choice, he just had to pursue it.

His blood was on fire.

5

Brenton Granger had not actually called the election, but it was definitely in the air. Even though he had not said a word publicly, Arthur Cramp, generally known in the party as 'Uncle Arthur', being his lone confidant, everyone was talking about its imminence as if they had special, private knowledge.

Many even alleged they knew the day on which the election would be held, and several different dates were being advanced with equal conviction. Some were even predicting the number of seats the party would win in such a contest and, further, which of the winning members would then be going into the cabinet.

One reason an election was imminent, the soothsaysers and prophets insisted, was that Granger had arranged this large event in a local hotel, the guests were all friends of his, and it was being paid for entirely out of party funds. Were the election not just around the corner, they argued, Granger would have invited a greater diversity of political opinion and staged the event in the Red Room at Province House.

Gathered in this cavernous, garishly lighted, tasteless ballroom, were several hundred of the party's leading supporters, all of them keyed up and ready for the fight. They wondered if they would hear from the premier's own lips today when the trumpet would sound for action.

Naturally, the centre of attention was Granger himself, looking healthy and handsome, his eyes shining, his silver hair flashing, his smile everlasting. He was flanked by his wife Florence, a frail but dignified woman; his son, Anthony, a dark-browed, rather arrogant looking young man of twenty-six; and his beautiful twenty-year-old twin daughters, Poppy and Petra. Behind them, basking in reflected glory, hovered Ernest Maddingly, benign and solicitous; and Sam MacNeil, the party treasurer, of whom it was said that when he was the Collector of Municipal Rates for the former County of Halifax, the funds had been substantially oversubscribed.

Not far away, leaning against the wall of an alcove, never taking his eyes off the premier for a second, was Reg Parsons, the premier's chauffeur, an enigmatic, shifty, figure with small, black, darting eyes, who, in one capacity or another, had been with Granger for years, long before he had even gone into politics.

Parsons had little time for anyone other than his boss, and nobody had any time for him. That was the way he liked it. He had no small talk, was certainly not inclined to gossip, and heartily disliked people in general. For those he imagined had insulted or damaged Granger in any way, he bore a malicious grudge, never forgiving and never forgetting. And for anyone who, believing Parsons had the ear of the premier, went out of their way to be friendly towards him, he had nothing but the heartiest contempt.

To say that Parsons was disliked and distrusted by all was no exaggeration, but nobody dared treat him with anything but respect, and very few even dared say a negative word about him. Although when somebody once remarked that Parsons was "as loyal as a dog" to Granger, Zandili Joseph had replied, "That's most appropriate for a cur like him."

In the outer regions of the ballroom, various groups were talking, clinking glasses, and generally congratulating themselves on what they were sure would be another resounding success at the polls, even though none knew when it would be.

Tom, together with his twenty-three-year old son, Andrew, was talking with Uncle Arthur Cramp, Stephanie Gilmour, Wendell

Proctor and his lady friend, Cynthia Smith, a sophisticated, stylishly dressed white woman in her late thirties. Intruding into this circle was Zandili Joseph, loudly complaining.

Zandili, who had actually been christened Mary, was a woman in her forties, dressed in a brightly coloured African outfit. She was constantly complaining; about what, her friends were not always sure and, truth to tell, they often just stopped listening, allowing her to ramble on.

Cramp, hunched and craggy, listened to the prattle with amusement. He had seen and heard it all many times before, and he found it fascinating how often, and how precisely, history repeated itself. With a few changes to the individuals and what they were wearing, he could recall identical conversations ten, twenty and thirty years before. He nodded from time to time, but spoke little. When he did speak, people stopped talking and listened intently.

In any company, Wendell would have stood out by virtue of his good looks, his ebullient personality, his height and his blackness. All eyes travelled to him instinctively, and when he laughed, as he often heartily did, it was difficult not to laugh along with him.

Tom and he had been the fastest of friends ever since Wendell had become an MLA in the campaign following Tom's by-election win. They were almost like brothers, constantly confiding in one another, and greatly enjoying each other's company.

Tom had been one of the first to learn about Wendell's attraction to, and successful pursuit of Cynthia. It was abundantly clear from how they looked each other and how they touched that Wendell and Cynthia were very much in love, but in their case the course of true love was not at all running smoothly.

Not far away from this circle was Wendell's sister, Grace, with her husband, Matthew. Grace was an imposing, tall, attractive, forceful woman in her forties who suffered no opposition to her opinions on any subject. Matthew, on the other hand, was a very large man, awkward and out of place in this and most other settings; but he had a huge heart and was kindness itself to anyone who was fortunate enough to make his acquaintance. So different were their temperaments, the couple were often described as being like "chalk and cheese" or "night and day".

Glaring disapprovingly at Cynthia, Grace sharply nudged Matthew, drawing his attention to what she regarded as neither appropriate nor desirable. Uneasy, Matthew moved away from her, anxious to avoid a public expression of what had hitherto been privately aired opinions on Wendell's relationship with the white woman. Had you asked her, Grace would have said it had nothing to do with prejudice, only with the fact that Cynthia was "snobby", would never fit in with the family, and that Grace knew plenty of suitable black women with whom Wendell might be well matched.

At the far end of the ballroom, as yet unseen by Tom, Heidi, glass in hand, was trapped in a corner by George Reynolds, a balding man in his fifties who was clearly inebriated. Red-faced and insistent, he must have imagined that Heidi liked him, mistakenly interpreting her sweet smile and patience for reciprocal interest, so he continued to pester her, gesticulating expansively. She desperately wanted to escape from what she was sure would soon become his clutches, but she knew he was one of her father's largest financial contributors.

Two overdressed, middle-aged women, members of what Uncle Arthur called "the blue rinse brigade," observed this awkward situation.

"Look at old Reynolds," snapped the first woman, "making a fool of himself with that young girl. How could he possibly think she could be interested in him?"

"Even if she was interested," said the other woman, "how could it ever work?"

Back in Tom's circle, Uncle Arthur was pressed to give his opinion. "We should be able to get back in," he said. "At least one of the opposition leaders shouldn't be a problem."

"I hear Smethwick is raising a ton of money," said Stephanie.

"I don't care if he owns Fort Knox," snarled Cramp. "The guy's a refugee from The Three Stooges."

Tom and Wendell laughed. They were both extremely fond of Uncle Arthur and appreciated his occasional witticisms.

Over the others' shoulders, Tom could see Brenton Granger glad-handing his way across the room like a typhoon of conviviality.

"I tell you, Art, I'm not a bit happy about Granger climbing on the Family Values bandwagon," chimed in Zandili.

"What do you care, Zandili?" Cramp said acidly. "So long as you get handouts for the layabouts and lesbians in your constituency, you'll like it or lump it."

Zandili's eyes flashed with rage, but before she could retaliate, Granger burst upon them, overflowing with strength and confidence. "My happy warriors from the House!" He oozed bonhomie. "With troops like these, who would shy away from any battle?"

He put an arm around Cramp's shoulders and said, "Good to see you, Art."

Then he grabbed Stephanie and kissed her cheek. "Stephanie, you're looking lovely as usual."

Seizing Tom's hand, he said, "Tom! How are you?"

"Fine, thank you, Premier. This is my son, Andrew."

"Andrew! What a name! The patron saint of bonny Scotland. Are you going to follow your old man into politics?"

"Not a chance, I..."

But Granger had already lost interest and, uttering a well-practised, hearty laugh, he punched Andrew on the arm and turned to Wendell.

"Wendell! I can see you're in great shape. And Cynthia!" He took her hand and kissed it. "Cynthia, my dear, how very nice of you to grace us with your presence."

"Brent," chipped in Uncle Arthur, "it looks like everyone is gonna vote for the party. Only Zandili here is still a little shaky."

Granger grabbed her and, giving her an exaggerated hug, loudly kissed her on the lips.

Although still angry with Cramp for having embarrassed her, Zandili tittered like a little girl. She was quite a different woman, quieter and much more deferential, with the man who had the ultimate power to dispense advancement and patronage.

"You know you can rely on me, Premier," she said, almost curtsying.

"Sure I do!" Then in an altogether more serious tone, "Art, I need to talk to you. The rest of you, circulate. Find out whose griping and report back to Art. I need to know if we have any traitors lurking in the bushes. Any snakes in the grass. Worms under the rocks."

As Granger ushered Cramp away, Cynthia, Stephanie and Zandili obediently mingled with the crowd. Tom, Wendell and Andrew accepted fresh drinks from a passing waiter.

Across the room, Heidi, having finally gotten rid of Reynolds, spotted Tom and slowly made her way towards him.

"Zandili does have a point," Wendell said to Tom. "This Family Values stuff can be a double-edged sword."

"Well, Granger's clean. Anyone can see he's the perfect family man," said Tom.

"Who's the babe, Dad?" asked Andrew, inclining his head in Heidi's direction.

Turning, Tom was taken by surprise to see Heidi approaching. Obviously glad to see him, she flashed a huge smile. Tom could hardly breathe and felt as if he was about to drop dead, his heart was pounding so hard in his chest.

"Hi! Remember me? From the audition?"

33

"Yes...yes...of course I do," Tom stammered, "Hello. What are you doing here?"

"I came to give Dad a boost."

"Yes, of course you did." Not knowing what else to say, Tom turned quickly to Andrew and Wendell, who were looking at him very strangely.

"Heidi, this is my son, Andrew. And this is my friend, Wendell Proctor."

"Mr. Proctor, I've heard a lot about you from my dad—all good."

"I'm glad to hear that," said Wendell.

"Hi Andy," said Heidi, playfully bumping into him, "Are you going to come and see me in your dad's play?"

Andrew did not answer, but just stood gazing spellbound at Heidi.

"Andrew. Answer the lady."

"Er...sure...when is it?"

"Not for a month yet. We've only just started rehearsals."

"Okay," Andrew said with conviction, "You bet. I'll be there."

Heidi gave him an enormous smile. Andrew smiled back at her.

"You bringing culture to the masses again, Tom?" asked Wendell.

"I'm trying. I should say, *we* are trying," Tom said, indicating Heidi.

"Yes, *we* are trying," said Heidi, "I must go and find the family now. It was lovely to meet you all."

"You too, Heidi," said Andrew.

As Tom watched her glide away from them, he was distracted from his beguilement by the sight of Brenton Granger and Arthur Cramp huddled in the corner, clearly deep in confidential conversation. The hearty humour and buoyant spirits which had been evident on their faces earlier had disappeared.

6

After the reception, Tom drove Andrew home to his apartment in the city's north end. Andrew had left Sydney Mines and come to Halifax several years ago. He had first found the place when he went to Dalhousie University because it was cheap. After graduating, he stayed because he thought he should live in the community he served, as he somewhat piously put it.

Andrew was a lawyer, but he went almost directly from law school to the university's legal aid clinic on Gottingen Street, where he had been for only a few months, his sole experience in private practice having been his articles.

Doing relatively low-paid legal work for the poor and needy tended to give him notions of his own importance in the world considerably greater than was warranted by the facts. It also, Tom had to admit, made Andrew rather self-righteous and judgmental, holding Tom and his colleagues responsible for all of society's problems, and somehow suggesting that if he and his kind were in power they would have them quickly solved.

Tom loved his son dearly, but often found him a bit tiresome, especially for the sanctimonious way in which he dismissed any person Tom could propose as an enemy of the working class. "Sell out", "puppet" and "bourgeois careerist" were among Andrew's favourite terms for describing almost everybody outside his own immediate circle. These epithets he dispensed freely and indiscriminately.

Andrew also seemed to regard Tom's occupation as an MLA as something less than decent, often making cheap jokes about the legislature and its occupants. Although, strangely enough, he did have some respect for Brenton Granger, whom he saw as someone who knew what he wanted and was determined to get it.

Tom could never understand this apparent contradiction, and put it down to the magnetic attraction a person with power has for those who have little or none.

He pulled up outside the old apartment building, but kept the car running. "I won't come in, Andy, because I have to go check the lighting rig at the theatre."

"Why do you do all this theatre stuff, anyway?" Andrew asked. "Don't you get enough drama down in the funny farm where you work?"

"This is a different kind of drama. I have more control over this."

"I think you just do it to try to get babes," Andrew said with a snigger.

"I wish."

"Well, that Heidi is certainly something else. Wow! I sure wouldn't mind taking a run at her."

"Yes, she is rather nice," said Tom. He winced, horrified at the way Andrew was talking about the object of his affection; as if Heidi were just like any other woman.

"Yep. Think I may take a run at her," Andrew repeated.

"I wouldn't advise it," said Tom seriously, "considering who she is."

"Huh! If I want to, I will. You won't stop me." Andrew snorted. "See you, Pops."

He jumped out of the car, slammed the door and bounded up the outside stairs to his apartment.

If, earlier in the day, Tom Aldridge had been enthusiastic and optimistic about the days ahead, he no longer felt that way.

7

Heidi shared an apartment on the top floor of an old house which had once been the home of a prosperous merchant's family. Clearly, its better days were now behind it. What had once been a spacious, elegant residence had been divided and subdivided many times in order to cram as many tenants—and the concomitant income therefrom—into the available space.

In the apartment, the furniture, none of it in peak condition and now strewn with articles of clothing, had been brought from different previous places, so there was no coordination as to style or colour. Various family mementos and university photographs adorned the plain, stained walls, together with posters of the Colosseum, the Eiffel Tower, and the Tuscan hills. In other words, the apartment had all the signs of being a convenient, temporary dwelling for people who shortly hoped to be settled in a more salubrious place.

At least, that was Heidi's view of the place, and as soon as she received the promotion she was expecting at the bank where she worked, she intended to get a much nicer crib than this one. She knew that she could always get financial assistance from her father, who had been well paid as a neurosurgeon before becoming premier, or her mother, who had brought inherited wealth to the marriage, but she was resolved to be as independent as possible.

She could have eased her budget considerably by dropping by the family home at meal times and eating free, but she did not feel as comfortable there as she had in the past.

She had no problem with her mother, who was as sweet as she was wise, and when Heidi could find her alone, they had some wonderful conversations about life, love and the world around them. However, she found her sisters, the twins, to be excessively silly now they had recently left their teens, spending all their time looking at their cell phones or prattling about clothes. Added to which, they had the annoying habit of talking at the same time, creating the impression of there being an echo in the room.

Then there was her brother, Anthony, who was at medical school, intending to follow in his father's footsteps, and who, she had to admit, could be a royal pain in the buttocks. For whatever reason, Anthony behaved like a man three times his age, unusually stern, forever censorious, and constantly treating Heidi as if she were a little girl with no propriety and even less sense.

Had he acted this way towards the twins, Heidi could have understood and easily forgiven him, but to Poppy and Petra he was invariably encouraging, considerate and affectionate.

Consequently, Heidi spent rather more time in the apartment than she wished to, which in turn meant having to talk to her roommate, Leslie, more often and for longer than was either edifying or entertaining.

Leslie was an Asian-Canadian of twenty-eight, with long, jet-black hair, who never dressed in anything but black and drank more wine than was good for her. Leslie was good-looking in a rather serious, almost sour, way and she attempted to exert a protective influence over Heidi, more often and more strongly than the latter found congenial. Heidi had often wondered if Leslie's interest in her was of a sexual nature, but nothing had ever been said, and no move had been made, to confirm her suspicions.

Today, they were being visited by Francine, a red-haired, loud, somewhat scatterbrained childhood friend of Heidi's. They were discussing—as they often did—men, and in particular Heidi's former boyfriend, Trevor, with whom she had recently broken up, not least because of Leslie's constant disparagement of him.

"I'm glad you see that we were right about Trevor," said Leslie.

"Face it, Heidi," said Francine, "the guy's a dork."

"Yes," Heidi agreed. "I didn't always think so, but I wish I had listened to you earlier. He was very immature. And now he's become a real pest."

"He been bothering you again?" Leslie inquired.

"Yes. He's not exactly stalking me, but he knows what time I get off work and is sometimes waiting for me."

"Creep! What's his excuse?"

"He says I should reconsider my breaking up with him because he has changed." Heidi said.

"Changed! They never change, because they never grow up!" Leslie asserted.

"Don't tell me you still miss the little shit," said Francine.

"Well, not him. I miss...well, you know what..."

"Jesus!" snapped Leslie. "They're none of them any good. Not even for that."

"Well, ladies," said Francine, getting up, "I must love you and leave you. I can't spend all night listening to your true confessions. I've got a date with the hunk."

"Not the footballer again?" asked Leslie with obvious distaste.

"That's him. I know he doesn't have much going on in his head, but he's sure got it in other places."

Heidi laughed, but Leslie was clearly not amused. She grabbed a cushion and flung it at Francine. "Go! Get out of here, slut!"

Cackling gleefully, Francine gathered up her belongings and tripped away down the stairs.

After they heard Francine's footsteps fade away, Leslie kicked the door shut and turned to Heidi. "You staying in tonight?"

"Yes, I've got to start learning my lines for the play."

"I'm glad Francine didn't move in with us," Leslie said. "It's much better with just the two of us."

"Francine's okay. You're too hard on people, Leslie. Trevor, for instance. He isn't half as bad as you make out. Not that I'm going back with him, or anything like that. I want to keep myself free."

The instant the words were out of her mouth, she regretted them, realizing that Leslie would pounce.

"Free for what?" Leslie demanded. "For who?"

"Oh, nothing."

"Nothing my ass! Come on, out with it."

"A guy I met. I don't really know. It might be something."

"Tell me about him."

"No, I don't want to talk about it. I don't even know if I like him."

"Oh, you like him, alright," insisted Leslie. "Otherwise you wouldn't be talking about keeping yourself free."

"Maybe. I don't know if he likes me."

"Heidi," said Leslie, her tone suddenly changing from severe to tender, "of course he likes you. Who wouldn't like you? You're the easiest person to fall in love with that I ever met."

"Gee, thanks Les," said Heidi, not entirely sure of the full meaning of Leslie's comments. "Anyway, I must get on and learn these lines."

8

The weeks went by, the weather got warmer, and rehearsals for the St. Michael's Players production of *The Rehearsal* ground on, with a great deal of time being spent on the boring but necessary business of blocking—deciding the most appropriate movements and positions of the actors in each scene.

Heidi received her promotion at the bank—she was now an assistant manager—but decided not to move from her apartment until the play was over and done with, and her head was clearer. When not working at the bank, she was preoccupied with her role in the play, but she could not avoid frequently, but surreptitiously, glancing at Tom during rehearsals and wondering what, if anything, existed between them.

For his part, Tom was still in an agitated state, and was becoming increasingly enamoured, feasting his eyes on her every movement on the stage. He knew he would have to make a move soon, but did not know how or when.

First, he came to the conclusion that if anything was to happen, it would be better for it to happen naturally, at the right time and under the right circumstances. Then, he wondered if that course of action was just cowardice, and that something more precipitous was called for. The truth was, he just could not make up his mind.

One evening, the sun's rays were slanting dramatically through the tall, arched windows, catching specks of dust in the columns of light. They had been rehearsing for over an hour and a certain lethargy had descended on the proceedings.

Marge was at the edge of the stage, script in hand, checking that the actors were in the right places at the right times. Phemie sat at her table at the centre of the hall, gently tapping her pen on her clipboard. Scattered around the auditorium sat several of the cast, waiting to make their entrances.

Tom lounged in the front row to the left of the aisle, the script on his knee revealing that he had been doodling again, this time drawing a series of small angels. Had he allowed anyone to examine them carefully, they would have discovered that they all looked like Heidi.

On stage, Heidi and Leonard were rehearsing their roles as Lucille and the Count. Already, they both knew many of their lines and only occasionally needed to glance down at their scripts.

> Leonard: *What will this paragon do? Talk about the moon? Throw himself on his knees, pounding himself on the chest?*
> Heidi: *He'll be shy. I don't suppose he'll say a word.*

She glanced at Tom, who caught her eye then quickly looked away.

> Heidi: *He may even avoid my eyes. He may ask another girl to dance, but I shall know that I'm the one he really loves.*

"Lovely. Beautiful. Let's move on," called Tom. "Can we have Hero, Eliane, Hortensia, Villebosse, and Damiens on stage please."

As David, Dorothy, Ingrid, Hugh and Earl, the actors playing the characters Tom had listed, trooped on to the stage, Marge switched on the overhead lights and suddenly the brighter light made the place seem more cheerful.

"Let's do the 'Yes, yes,' bit first," Tom said. "Go, Leonard."

Leonard and Heidi took up their positions again.

Leonard: *Yes, yes. You say all that very well.*

Leonard moved to Heidi, touching her lightly with one hand.

"No! No! Leonard, not like that." Tom exclaimed. "This is the Count's first chance to get close to Lucille. To touch her. Put an arm right around her. Get as close as you can."

He leapt onto the stage to demonstrate how he wanted the action to appear. He draped his left arm round Heidi's shoulders, his hand resting on her upper arm. Her warmth and softness momentarily unnerved him and he froze.

Heidi felt his hesitation and gently snuggled into him, so that when his right hand pointed to the passage in the script she was almost enveloped by him.

For a split second, Tom was in a dream, then he snapped out of it and quickly stepped back. "See that, Leonard? That's the way to do it."

When Heidi gazed at Tom, she smiled, and their eyes engaged. They were still looking at each other when, down on the floor, Phemie raised her eyebrows to Marge, who slowly shook her head.

9

When he attended St. Francis Xavier University, Tom met a man who befriended him and with whom he had been in touch ever since. Blaine Dixon came originally from Harcourt, New Brunswick and was also studying Business Administration. He and Tom had immediately hit it off, and they spent many hours in each other's company.

It was at college that Blaine had introduced Tom to community theatre. They joined a local group and got involved, at first taking minor roles or assisting behind the scenes.

Tom was bitten by the bug and had been dabbling in amateur theatrics ever since. After leaving university, Blaine moved to the United States, joined a large clothing supply company, and rose through the ranks to become its chief executive officer.

Once a month, usually on a Sunday, they would talk on the telephone for about an hour, their discussions ranging from world affairs to personal problems. So, on Sunday following the rehearsal of the play, Tom rushed home, bursting to share his news and knowing that Blaine would be receptive and might offer sound advice.

Tom's apartment, though well furnished, was modest, with a single bedroom and small kitchen. It was apparent that he spent little time here, because the apartment was rather too clean and tidy for a single man who used it as anything more than a place to sleep.

Apart from a photograph of Andrew on top of the television, there was little ornamentation of any kind, and the walls were bare. A small oasis of lived-in disorder was confined to the area around his favourite La-Z-Boy armchair, against which were piled a variety of books Tom intended to read if and when he found the time.

In contrast, Blaine Dixon lived in a splendid, huge, studio apartment in New York City, which was illuminated by light pouring in through the large windows. On the one wall which was not punctuated by windows hung large paintings by contemporary artists. The furniture was exquisite and expensive, and the carpets were thick and luxurious. To one side, a temperature-controlled wine closet revealed bottles of Bordeaux chateaux, some thirty years old, and a polished rosewood cabinet boasted a series of rare, single malt Scotch whiskies.

Blaine was the same age as Tom but, while he had a similar flicker of amusement about his lips, he was greyer and more lined. Where Tom was solid, Blaine was lithe, finely chiselled and, to some extent, willowy. He was also single, which, together with his appearance, had occasionally led to speculation about his orientation.

After they exchanged the usual pleasantries about health and work, Tom could contain himself no longer and blurted out the story of his infatuation for Heidi, including a fulsome description of her, the circumstances of their meeting, and his indecision about how to proceed.

"Sounds wonderful," said Blaine. "So, what's the problem?"

"She's kind of young."

"What, thirty, forty, something like that? That's nothing these days."

"Twenty four, I think," said Tom quietly.

"Holy cow! What are we talking about here, old pal?" Blaine

asked. "Anything more than firm, young flesh?"

"Yes, I think so. No, I *know* so."

"And what else? Does she smile a lot and give you funny looks?"

"Yes, that kind of thing. What do you think my chances are?"

"With twenty-plus years separating you, I'd say the odds were eighty/twenty against. Maybe not even that good."

"There's something else," said Tom, "she's the premier's daughter."

"Jesus! Isn't he your boss?" Blaine became serious. "Look, whatever you do, for God's sake play it very carefully. Don't try to force it. She has to come to you. Don't go rushing in with both feet."

"That's what I was thinking."

"And, Tom, please, don't fall in love with her," Blaine said sternly.

"I think I already have," Tom replied.

10

About the same time as Blaine and Tom were talking that Sunday, the Proctor family were gathered for dinner. Wendell's mother, Blossom, and his father, Douglas, were present, together with his sister, Grace, her husband, Matthew, and Wendell's Aunt Angela, Douglas's sister, and her husband, Graham.

The only person who was conspicuous by her absence was Cynthia, because she had not been invited.

Wendell strenuously objected to Cynthia's exclusion, but was determined not to say anything publicly about it because he wanted to avoid a shouting match over the Sunday roast. His plan was to get his mother alone in the kitchen and quietly ask her what had caused this egregious omission. Other than that, Wendell was resolved not to say anything which might provoke references to Cynthia, and he devoutly hoped others, particularly Grace, would do the same.

Shortly after everyone was seated, and drinks were being poured and circulated, his mother went to check on the vegetables, so Wendell slipped away from the table and followed her.

"Hey, Momma," he said quietly so as not to be overheard in the next room, "can I have a quick word?"

"I'm kind of busy, son, as you can see," Blossom said defensively, guessing what was on Wendell's mind.

"It won't take long, and you can carry on doing stuff while we talk."

"Well, what is it?" Blossom did not like to be cornered.

"Why didn't you invite Cynthia tonight?"

"No particular reason."

"'No particular reason'?" Wendell mimicked his mother's tone. "You know she is practically my fiancée."

"Not yet," said his mother flatly.

"But she soon will be! You can count on it!"

"Don't you raise your voice to your mother. I don't care if you are some fancy cabinet minister."

"Come on, Ma," said Wendell lowering his volume. "What's the story?"

"Your father and I thought—"

"Don't be implicating Dad. This is Grace's work, isn't it?"

"Well..."

"I thought so. What's she been saying?"

"Just stuff about her never being able to fit in with us ordinary people."

"That's crazy, Momma." Wendell insisted. "Cynthia is ordinary people,"

"Wendell, leave me be. I mean, I don't really know the woman."

"And you're not likely to if you never invite her over."

"Leave me be, I say! Go and sit down. Your dinner will be out any minute."

When Wendell returned to the table he was more than a little annoyed because, some days ago, when he had asked his mother if she would ask Cynthia to dinner, she had replied, "Oh sure," in an off-hand manner. He sat down hoping that, at least, the rest of the occasion could be carried on with civility.

"Wendell," called Douglas from the end of the table, "I poured you a beer, but I can get you wine if you prefer it."

"No thanks, Dad. Beer is fine," said Wendell. He reached out for the glass and took a sip.

"I'm surprised your tastes haven't become more elevated, considering the rarefied circles you move in these days," said Grace.

"Seems to me you and Matt were moving in those circles yourselves not long back," Wendell said with a grin, referring to Granger's party at the hotel. He noticed that Matthew was also smiling slightly.

Just then, Blossom brought in an enormous prime rib and set it down in front of her husband. Douglas took up the carving knife and deliberately honed it on an old steel which, from its appearance, had been in the family for generations.

Then Blossom brought in mountains of potatoes, roasted and mashed, cabbage and carrots, followed by a huge jug of gravy. Douglas carefully carved slices of medium rare meat, placing them on big, flower-printed plates which were passed hand to hand around the company.

They soon set to, munching away happily in silence. From time to time, Blossom invited them to have seconds, and then thirds, until everyone had eaten far more than they intended.

"Momma, another masterpiece," Wendell announced. "One of your very best."

"First class!" Douglas said. "Did you have enough, Matthew?"

"Sure did," replied Matthew, though from the size of him, he still looked as if he had room for more.

"Lovely meal, Blossom," said Angela.

"Great," said Graham, who, like Matthew, was a man of very few words when his wife was present.

"My heaven, Wendell, you sure cleaned your plate," said Grace.

"Two plates," Wendell corrected.

"Must be a come-down from some of the fancy food you get downtown."

"Let it go, Grace," Wendell warned.

"I mean, I'm sure you go to quite a few expensive restaurants with that woman."

"She has a name, Grace."

"Oh yes, what is it now? Cynthiah." Grace pronounced it in a la-di-da manner.

Everyone, especially the men, looked uncomfortable and started to shift in their seats. Matthew gently put his hand on Grace's arm, but she quickly brushed it off.

"That's right," said Wendell. Then, unable to stop himself, he added, "The woman I intend to marry."

"Well, that gets us right to the point, doesn't it?" Grace said defiantly. "Your family thinks you are making a mistake and they want to save you from it."

"I don't need saving, especially not by you."

"Oh, listen to that! Somebody has to do something. It's for your own good."

"I notice that Grace is the only one doing any talking," Wendell observed. "Do you all feel the way she does? How about you, Dad?"

Douglas looked down at the table, tracing patterns with his spoon.

"And you, Graham?"

"Leave me out of it," Graham said hastily.

"Matt?"

"I keep my opinions to myself," said Matt quietly. "Grace does more than enough talking for the both of us."

"Auntie Angela? What about you?"

"Well, I think you should listen to your mother."

"And we all know what she thinks. Or what she thinks since Grace brainwashed her."

At this, the table erupted, Blossom expressing hurt outrage, the men growling, Angela tut-tutting, and Grace booming with righteous indignation.

"We all know what this is about. It's about Cynthia being white," said Wendell bitterly as he rose from the table. "It would seem most of you are bigots, and some of you are racists!"

He rapidly exited, leaving howls of anger and resentment behind him. Never was the calm of the street as welcome as it was now.

11

Here in the suburbs, the new leaves were adorning the trees and the night was soft, warm and inky blue. From a nearby park and the adjacent gardens, the sound of frogs peeping overrode the muted noise of traffic from the city. Behind safely curtained bay windows, comforting, pink light gently seeped through chinks in the heavy, expensive material, and over some porches, fake Victorian lanterns twinkled with pretension.

Most dwellings on this street were individual houses of some size, each with an expansive garden in which early flowers were coming into bloom. All had elaborate, fairly modern garages, some with space for more than one vehicle. This *cul de sac* was not a place for the poor, or even the middle incomes; it was a haven for those who had succeeded and planned to keep hold of their wealth and positions.

One building on the street was different from the others. It was a small, three-story apartment building of a superior sort, save for the fact that its fire escape was visible from the road, and was tacked onto the side, marring the structure's otherwise rather elegant appearance. This building was largely occupied by people of advanced age and quite substantial means, with widows being the predominant tenants.

The end of the street where the apartment building was situated was also the shadiest part of the street, there being only one street lamp here and eight very large trees directly across the road, which backed on to the park. Three were eastern white pine, three were red maples and the remaining two were an elm and a Peking willow.

In the resultant darkness, barely visible, was a silent, black limousine, lurking in its own stench of gasoline and warm rubber. Sitting silently at the wheel, and smoking out of the open window, was Reginald Parsons, the premier's chauffeur. He had been here many times before, but was never bored, never impatient. It was his job, his vocation, to wait and serve, and he was more than happy to do it without question or complaint.

If pressed by the right people, Parsons would have been the first to admit that he was a nobody, and that it served his purposes that everyone should regard him as such. From a dysfunctional, alcoholic family in Rockdale, a small rural community in Richmond County, he was a small, scrawny man with no formal education, and little to commend him to others, and definitely not his querulous temper and sour, vindictive personality.

His past was murky and not completely recorded, but included convictions for a number of petty crimes and a few which were highly unsavoury. He was illiterate and had few pleasures apart from smoking, drinking rum—but only when off duty—and a monthly visit to a prostitute on Water Street named Naiomi.

If Parsons had a redeeming quality, it was that he was loyal, but loyal only to one man, Brenton Granger. He saw Granger almost as a superman, if not a god, head and shoulders above the crowd, but never properly appreciated, never receiving the thanks Parsons felt he so richly deserved. For Granger he would do anything.

Years before, more than twenty now, Parsons had been diagnosed with a particularly delicate and complex case of Arteriovenous Malformation in his brain, a highly abnormal tangle of blood vessels, connecting arteries and veins, which was severely disrupting blood flow and the circulation of oxygen. He had gone through doctors who knew little and understood even less about his condition, and was eventually referred to specialists. By then, Parsons was in a bad way and was not expected to live. At that time, there were few surgeons who could perform the necessary operation, and those who could opined that it would be too complicated to take the risk, and that he would die one way or the other.

Except Brenton Granger, who had examined him and taken pity on the little man, not knowing quite why. He explained to Parsons that his chances of survival were very slight, but he was prepared to undertake the task of trying to untangle the mess in his brain. He said it would be even more difficult than trying to sort out the individual strands in a pot of cooked spaghetti after it had been hurled against a wall.

Granger had even gone to battle for Parsons with the hospital authorities, and then the Department of Health, both of which wanted to stop the operation on the grounds of its impracticability and expense, and he prevailed.

And, contrary to all predictions, the operation was a success. So much so that, within several months, Parsons had been fully restored to normal health.

Parsons was so grateful that he kept showing up at Granger's offices, offering his services to his saviour, even for no compensation if that was what it took to convince the surgeon of his devotion.

Granger was touched, and took Parsons on as a handyman around the office for a nominal wage. In time, he discovered that, although Parsons was neither numerate nor literate, he had an extraordinary knack for organization, and eventually Granger made him office manager. Later, when Granger went into politics, it seemed only natural that Parsons would follow him.

Although he would never have claimed to fully understand Parsons and his motives, Granger knew that he was the one man in the entire world on whom he could rely under all circumstances, and that as such he needed to keep him close.

Parsons was keeping a beady eye on a window of a third-story apartment, which he knew Granger had visited many times before, sometimes as often as twice a week. He was suddenly alerted from his torpor by a vision of Granger and a woman appearing at the window, apparently arguing quite violently.

Parsons hitched himself up on the edge of his seat as Granger, apparently remonstrating unsuccessfully with the woman, gave up and disappeared, only seconds later to reappear on the fire escape and descend rapidly to the street.

Parsons started the car and prepared to move off when he noticed the woman looking out of the window and another figure—a man's—appearing behind her.

Granger opened the door, sat down and buckled his safety belt.

"Come on, Reg. Let's go."

"Okay, boss," said Parsons. "Something wrong?"

"Yeah. She's changed a lot lately. Seems I can't do enough for her. I don't understand it."

"I guess it had to happen sooner or later, boss. You know what they're like."

"Yes, I know, but we've been together for years," said Granger, almost like a little boy who had lost a favourite toy, "You know that. I can no longer figure out what she wants."

"Boss, maybe I shouldn't mention this, but..."

"What? Go on."

"Just as you was comin' down the fire escape, I seen someone come up behind her. A man."

"What?" Granger seemed thunderstruck. "Are you sure? Are you absolutely sure, Reg?"

"Cross my heart and hope to die, boss."

Granger whistled through his teeth and clenched his fists. "So, that's it. She's going to put the squeeze on me."

"Dirty fuckers," said Parsons with absolute conviction. "What you gonna do?"

"Don't know yet. Let's see how much she wants first. If it's reasonable, I may be able to handle it."

"But you know she'll keep coming back for more, boss. You know that, don't you?"

"We'll see. Just drive me home, Reg. And thanks a lot for everything."

"That's what I'm here for," said Parsons, hunkering down behind the wheel. His weasel face wore a more than usually implacable and malignant expression.

12

As the Chief Whip of his Legislative caucus, Tom Aldridge had an office with a window, as opposed to back benchers, who merely shared partitioned spaces. True, it was not a very large window, but if he pushed his chair back a few feet and craned his neck he could get a glimpse of the small Legislature gardens with its lawn, flower beds, and a tree planted by XMLAS, the association of former members of the legislature.

The office was not very big, having room enough only for his desk, a clothing stand, and a chair for any person who might be coming to see him with a problem, or a colleague with a question about times and procedures.

Today, that chair was occupied by Andrew, who was in a particularly obstreperous mood, and was sprawled with one leg over the chair's arm and the other with a foot on Tom's desk. Tom was trying to get some work done, but Andrew had other ideas.

"I've been watching you the past couple of days, old man," he said portentously. "I know there's something going on."

"What do you mean, 'going on'? Like what?"

"Don't know. I can't put my finger on it."

"Well, you'd better keep your finger out of it."

"Ha, ha," Andrew sneered. "I wonder what it could be. What mysterious event has occurred?"

"Andrew, I've got a lot of work to do," Tom said seriously. "If there's nothing sensible you have on your mind, I'd be glad if you'd let me get on with it."

"Let me see," continued Andrew, ignoring his father. "I know. Maybe you've got the hots for some babe."

"I wish you wouldn't use language like that," said Tom, frowning.

"Bingo! So that is it!"

"What a smart ass you are."

"Let's have the scoop, Pops. Who is it?"

"If you must know, it's just someone who's in the play."

"She's married, huh? Is that why you're keeping mum?"

"No, don't be ridiculous. It's just that she's..."

"She's what?"

"Nothing. Please go away and let me get on with my work."

Andrew threw back his head and started to tap the arm of his chair. "Hmm. Let's see now...wait a minute...no, it can't be...we're not talking about Heidi, are we?"

"What if we are?"

"You're old enough to be her father, for Christ's sake! She could be my sister."

"Then she's very lucky she isn't."

"Jesus! I was going to call her myself. You couldn't give me her number, could you?"

"No I couldn't. And you keep your nose out of it."

"Like hell I will," said Andrew defiantly, "You don't own her. She's fair game. If she wants to go out with me, that'll be her decision."

At that Wendell poked his head around the door, interrupting them. Tom noticed, as he had many times before, that Wendell was so tall his head was only inches from the ceiling. Stephanie Gilmour was with him.

"Sorry, Tom. I didn't know you were tied up. Hi, Andy, how're you doing?"

"Fine, thanks, Wendell," said Andrew, still sprawling.

Neither Wendell nor Tom said anything, but just looked at him.

Andrew eventually took the hint. "Okay, okay, I was leaving anyway."

He grabbed his briefcase from the floor, brushed past Stephanie with a curt greeting, and stomped off down the corridor.

"Is he alright?' inquired Wendell.

"Yes, it's nothing. Hey, Stephanie! What can the humble Whip do for two distinguished cabinet ministers?"

"I don't know why Stephanie is here," said Wendell, "but I came to get that letter you said you'd got from one of my constituents."

"Oh, yes," said Tom, reaching into the desk drawer, "I don't know why the poor man wrote to me, but he obviously has one hell of a problem. Here it is."

"Thanks," said Wendell, taking the file. "Tom, we need to have a chat soon."

"Problems? "

"Sort of. It can wait."

"Okay. See you, Wendell. Come in, Stephanie."

Stephanie waited until Wendell could be heard retreating down the corridor, then sidled up to Tom's desk. She looked especially alluring today, with a classy new hairdo and a crisp, white summer dress.

"You alright, Tom? You look a little frazzled."

"I'm fine, thanks, Stephanie. What can I do for you?"

"It's going to be such a beautiful evening, I wondered if you'd like to come over for supper on the back porch."

"That sounds great, but I planned on working tonight. I have a lot to catch up on,"

"Oh," Stephanie sounded surprised that anyone could turn down such an invitation. "Well, how about tomorrow night?"

"Ah, sorry, I have rehearsals. I'm directing a new play at St. Mike's."

Stephanie came round the desk and put her hand on Tom's arm.

Tom smiled at her, not sure if this was more than a friendly gesture.

"How about the weekend?"

"More rehearsals. Saturday and Sunday."

"Okay Tom," Stephanie sighed softly. "I'll see you around."

When Stephanie had left, Tom, still upset by his altercation with Andrew, went to open the window. As he was raising the sash, he noticed the premier and Arthur Cramp, their heads almost touching, sitting under a tree in the garden, and he wondered what they could be talking about in such a conspiratorial way.

~

It was a spectacular day, with scarcely a cloud in the sky, although still a little chilly in the shade. Birds were cheerfully singing, competing with the laughter and chatter of passers-by and early tourists, but none of the joys of the season were apparent in the faces of Brenton Granger and Arthur Cramp and they sat on a bench under the trees. Some yards away, out of earshot, was Parsons leaning against a tree smoking.

Brenton had on his Toronto Maple Leaf jacket, but Cramp, as always, wore the three-piece Warren Cook suit he had bought at Colwell's in the 1970s, which still fitted him and was in excellent condition.

"Walk with me, Arthur," said Granger, getting up from the bench.

"Where'd you want to go, Brent?"

"Just around the yard here. Just to make sure that if anyone hears anything, they won't get enough to make sense of it."

"Okay," said Cramp wearily hauling himself up.

They walked very slowly, Parsons following at a discreet distance. Cramp jerked his head in the chauffeur's direction and raised an eyebrow at Granger.

"Parsons is okay. He knows everything."

"Alright," said Cramp, sounding surprised. "Shoot."

"Art, the long and the short of it is that some years ago I began an extramarital relationship with a woman—"

"How long ago?"

"About ten years."

"Alright. Go on."

"Well, until recently everything was good, very good indeed. She supplied me with what I haven't been able to get at home—I won't go into details, that would be disrespectful to Florence—and some peace and quiet, which I could never get at the house, with those scatty twins of mine and all their crazy, teeny-bopper friends hanging about the place."

"I've got the picture, Brent. You don't have to justify yourself to me," said Cramp. "What happened?"

"You understand that I have been providing this woman with a generous allowance, as it were, and she's been living in a very nice place she could never have afforded otherwise."

"Who is she, Brent?"

"Let's just call her Madame X for the time being, if you don't mind." Granger sounded a little irritated at being interrupted.

"Okay," replied Cramp coolly. He was less than pleased that the premier was holding information back from him.

"Anyway, a couple of weeks ago, things started to change. It was like she was inventing reasons for us to fall out. At first I thought she just wanted to leave, and was preparing the ground."

"And now?"

"I'm now convinced she is going to blackmail me. If I don't cough up, she'll go public and pick an inconvenient time to do it."

"Like a general election," Cramp suggested.

"Exactly. She must have got wind that I was thinking of going to the polls soon. God knows, maybe I even told her that myself."

The premier wiped his forehead with his handkerchief. "I may have. I can't remember now."

They had now done a complete circle of the small gardens, and now started again, this time in a counter-clockwise direction. Cramp took a look around to see who was about. He noticed Tom in his office window and gave a brief wave.

"Who're you waving to?" The premier asked, looking nervous.

"Just Tom Aldridge. He's up there in his office. Give him a wave, Brent."

Granger rapidly put on his game face, smiled broadly and waved heartily to Tom, who returned the gesture.

"What makes you so sure she's going to blackmail you?" asked Cramp.

"Just after I left the other night, and she was watching from the window, Parsons noticed a man came up behind her."

"Jesus. That means—"

"Yeah. That means it's probable the bastard was hiding in the apartment the whole time I was there, and more than likely that he took some photographs of us, of me."

"Hmm. You'll let me know if it turns out as you suspect. Particularly the amount involved?"

"Yes, of course."

The premier stopped walking and turned to face Cramp. "What do you think we should do?"

Cramp paused for several seconds, jingling coins in his pocket and, narrowing his eyes, looked up into the trees. Granger thought he could almost hear the wheels turning in his brain.

Finally Cramp sniffed, cleared his throat, and lowered his voice to a level which was barely audible. "Between you and me, we've got a lot of money in the slush fund. I mean a *lot* of money. Depending on what she asks for, whether her word can be trusted, and whether we decide to pay, I could dip into that without too much difficulty. Ordinarily, I would say we'd need every penny we can get for an election, but this time the polls all say it should be a relatively easy ride."

A woman with a small child had come into the garden and started to throw a red, rubber ball to him. Granger gave her a huge smile and winked at the little boy.

"Good. Thanks, Art. I knew I'd be able to rely on you."

"Always could. Always will."

He and Cramp shook hands, whereupon Granger kicked the ball to the boy, nodded to his mother, then strode back into Province House. Parsons followed him in, completely ignoring both mother and child.

Cramp stood watching them go, then he turned to face the statue of Joseph Howe, a former premier of Nova Scotia who had been a great champion for freedom of the press in the nineteenth century. He speculated on whether Howe, and other people in politics in those far-off days, also had secrets and scandals, and if they too had wily old men who fixed their problems for them.

Grunting from the effort, he lowered himself down onto the edge of the statue's plinth and put his head in his hands. He did not notice when the little boy's ball rolled between his feet, and so distracted was he that the lad had to ask several times to have it returned.

When Cramp absently picked it up and looked up to hand it back, the child stared into the deeply lined, jaded face of a very old, very tired man.

13

Tonight the auditorium was dark, the only illumination coming from the stage and a tiny light attached to Phemie's clipboard. Marge was at stage right, fiddling with some black curtains, while Dorothy, Hugh, David and Earl lounged in front-row seats, most of them wearing their Louis Quatorze costumes. To one side stood Father Geoffrey, benignly surveying the proceedings.

Leonard was striking up a pose at down stage right with Heidi opposite him at stage left. Leonard wore white stockings, buckled shoes, culottes, a gold surcoat and a waterfall of white lace at his throat.

Heidi's costume was undergoing last minute alterations, so she was still wearing a tee shirt and shorts, both of which were briefer and tighter than usual. Feeling somewhat self-conscious, she asked herself if these really were the first garments out of the drawer, or did she choose them deliberately so as to be more appealing to Tom? She was forced to admit it was the latter, and instantly felt a little ashamed. Still, there was nothing that could be done about it now. She would have to retrieve her modesty some other time.

Tom stood in the aisle between the front row seats, script under his arm. "Sorry, but I want to do that bit again. It's still not right. Leonard, Heidi, you must remember that this is kind of a culmination of all they want, all they have been looking forward to for a long time. It must happen almost like a volcano, so when you go toward each other, dive down slightly and then push up when you get together, so we get a kind of erupting quality. You understand?"

"Absolutely," said Heidi.

"I think so," said Leonard, frowning.

Leonard is such a slow, dull-witted fellow, thought Tom uncharitably, and he certainly does not deserve to have so many intimate scenes with Heidi. If only I had been able to cast myself in the role, he thought, Heidi and I would have given a mesmerizing performance.

"Okay. Let's try it again. Just the bit from 'will you agree?' Okay, go!"

> Leonard: *Will you agree to leave?*
> Heidi: *Of course not. Now, I would rather stay.*

They hesitated briefly, then, when Tom clapped his hands, rushed into each other's arms, embraced and kissed. Supremely jealous, Tom let the kiss linger for a few more seconds before calling them off.

"Excellent, Heidi," said Tom. "I see they have your dress ready, so will you go and get fitted now? Please be as quick as you can."

Heidi ran off stage left where Marge and Doris, the wardrobe mistress, were waiting for her. They hustled her away to the dressing room.

"Okay, folks, if I can have your attention, please," Tom called out. "I have a few notes while Doris and Marge get Heidi into costume. Overall, I think we're in pretty good shape. A bit ragged here and there, but not at all bad. The cues are still way too slow. There are long silences between one person's lines and the next person's lines. You must work on this. Pick up your cues!

"Please remember, Dress Rehearsal is in two days and there'll be no scripts and no prompting. If you forget your lines or lose your place, you'll just have to work it out. If it happens, help one another. Whoever does know the correct line or place, just jump in and bring the scene back on course. During the run, you will have Marge to prompt, but not at the Dress.

"We'll be starting the Dress an hour earlier than usual, so we can party afterwards at my place. It'll be a bit of a squeeze, but I think we can all get in. Oh yes, the food and booze will be free."

Hugh and Earl cheered loudly while David and Dorothy pounded their seats.

"I thought that announcement might meet with your approval," said Tom. "I should have known that—"

He was interrupted by a loud rustling sound from the stage as Doris, Marge and Heidi entered, the latter now wearing a gorgeous, long, low-cut, shimmering, white silk dress which hung open to the waist behind, revealing Heidi's naked back. Doris and Marge were following her, pinning, hemming and tucking as they made their way to centre stage.

Tom felt as if he had been struck by a thunderbolt, and just goggled at this enthralling spectacle.

"How's this, Tom? Will it do?" Marge asked.

"Beautiful," said Tom as if in a daze. "Absolutely beautiful."

"Does he mean the dress or the girl?" Phemie muttered.

Father Geoffrey, the only one who had overheard her from his position by the window, frowned and uneasily shook his head.

~

When Heidi got home, she found Leslie had just washed her hair and had a towel wrapped around her head like a turban. She was sitting at the table reading a magazine, but looked up sharply when Heidi entered.

"Good God," she said. "What are you wearing?"

"What do you mean, what am I wearing?" Heidi was defensive.

"Just a tee shirt and some shorts."

"When did you buy them—when you were sixteen?"

"What are you talking about, Leslie? I've had them for a while. So what?"

"Well, I've never seen you in those before," said Leslie with a sneer. "Looks like you've been on the game."

"What? Are you saying I look like a prostitute?" Heidi was horrified.

"Only saying what comes to mind. I can't help it if that's the way it appears."

"Well, thanks a frigging bunch, Leslie!"

"Sorry." Leslie shrugged. "Didn't mean to upset you. You just back from rehearsal?"

"Yes."

"How's it going?"

"Fine, thank you."

"You really seem to be enjoying it this time."

"I always enjoy doing a play," said Heidi.

"Yeah, but you really seem to be into this one. Like you have more invested in it."

"Yes," said Heidi. Then, after a pause, "I guess I do."

"Any particular reason?"

"Maybe. I'm not sure."

"What the hell does that mean?" demanded Leslie.

"I'm tired. I'm off to bed. I'll see you tomorrow."

Disturbed without knowing quite why, Leslie watched Heidi go into her room and close the door. She knew there was something going on. She just could not figure out what it was.

14

The night before the dress rehearsal Tom received a telephone call from Blaine, saying that he had just learned he had to attend a meeting in St. John's Newfoundland, and that the only flight he could get was from Newark with a stop-over in Halifax. Tom offered to come out to the airport, but Blaine said he had over three hours to kill and would come into the city to have lunch with Tom.

Tom had not seen Blaine for several years, although they had spoken on the telephone many times. Blaine was stylishly dressed in a full length Prada leather coat, blue Cesare Attolini mohair silk suit and Gucci calfskin shoes. He wore quite an assortment of jewellery and a Patek Phillipe watch.

Life was obviously materially rewarding for Blaine, but Tom was surprised to see how much he had aged. Despite their being the same age, Blaine's hair was turning white and he had deep lines in his face.

They met at a downtown hotel, where they took a window table overlooking a busy street. Before they ordered their meal, they had a drink, Blaine ordering a glass of champagne while Tom stuck to beer.

"I've got to get back by two-thirty. It's a complete bummer having to go to Newfoundland, I can tell you, and if it wasn't for getting a chance to see you, I'd really be put out."

"Well, I'm very glad to see you," said Tom. "We haven't had the chance to get together for a long time. How are you, pal?"

"Good," Blaine smiled, "Stressed somewhat, but as well as can be expected. How about you? You look very well."

"Do I?"

"Yes, you look like you've lost a dollar and found a hundred."

"Really, I wonder why?"

"I would imagine it has something to do with your great romance."

"Possibly," said Tom, grinning. "Anyone special in your life these days?"

"Yes to anyone, no to special," answered Blaine enigmatically. "What progress is there to report on your paramour?"

"Not much. It's going slowly. I've taken your advice and haven't made a move. I guess you could say I am trying to create an environment in which she might take the initiative."

"Quite right. As much as you might be inclined to do otherwise, you must take your time. It's crucial. You know that?"

"I do. Yes, absolutely. It's not easy, in fact it's damn difficult, but that's what I'm trying to do."

Suddenly, Tom grabbed Blaine's arm. Through the window he could see Heidi walking up the street with Leslie and Francine, on their way to lunch.

"Quick, Blaine, look. That's her!"

"Which one?"

"The one in the middle."

"Ahhh," Blaine sighed, "now I understand."

~

After he had said his goodbyes to Blaine and seen his taxi off, Tom went to his car, and made his way across town to St. Michael's for the early dress rehearsal. Apart from a few technical glitches like missed lighting cues, the performance went much better than he anticipated. Even Leonard surprised him by rising to the occasion in grand style, and the rest of the cast put their hearts and souls into it.

Of course Heidi was very good—no, she was superlative, spectacular, magical—and in her new dress she looked amazingly, breathtakingly beautiful.

After the curtain had come down and Tom had given the cast and crew a few notes, people dispersed. Still in costume, Heidi went outside for some fresh air and sat on the steps by the stage door.

Seeing her, Tim could not resist strolling over. "You were wonderful tonight," he said with wholehearted sincerity. "Absolutely wonderful."

"I wasn't that good." Heidi laughed, but was glad to get the praise. "If I was, it was because I had an amazing director."

Tom could not think of the right reply to this comment, so they just looked at each other in silence. At length, he thought of what seemed like a brilliant idea. "Did you come by bus this evening?"

"Yes, I always do."

"In that case, could I give you a drive to the party?"

"Sure, that would be great. Thank you."

"Only too happy to oblige," Tom said, hearing himself sound stodgy and old fashioned.

"Is the food going to be cold?" Heidi asked.

"No, I'm going to rustle up some chicken curry and Spaghetti Bolognese."

"In that case, can I help you cook? Please."

"Thanks," said Tom, grateful and amazed that things were going so well. "That would be great. You get changed and meet me out front. It's the blue Elantra."

"Okay. See you soon."

"Oh, and Heidi, try to be as quick as you can. I have to get there before the others, to open up."

"The only immorality is not to do what one has to do when one has to do it, "said Heidi with a smile, quoting the author of their play. "I'll be right there."

~

Tom and Heidi were in the kitchen, she slicing tomatoes for the salad, he chopping onions for the curry. The noise level was high as cast and crew members unwound in the tightly-packed living room. Every few minutes, someone came in to get wine or beer from the fridge.

"I see you've got poor Heidi working already, Tom," Dorothy said. "Heidi, you should tell him that slavery has been abolished."

"Don't worry about me, Dorothy," Heidi said with a laugh. "Actually I'm the slave driver here. If it wasn't for me telling him what to do, Tom would be hopeless."

Tom laughed, too. He could not explain it, but Heidi's unexpected reply made him feel tender and amatory. He utterly adored her speaking of him in that way.

Dorothy took the wine out of the fridge and, returning to the living room, brushed against Father Geoffrey who, with a glass of whisky in hand, was hovering in the doorway, an owlish eye cast in Tom's direction.

"You look lovely tonight," Tom said, when Dorothy had left. "Just amazing."

"Thank you, kind sir," Heidi said lightly.

"Why didn't you bring your boyfriend tonight?"

"I don't have a boyfriend."

"Oh, really?" said Tom, perhaps a little too happily. "I am surprised. I'd have thought you could have any man you wanted."

"I don't want just any man," said Heidi, blushing.

At this, Tom became acutely embarrassed and, looking around for a diversion, grabbed the bowl of salad and handed it to her.

"Er...could you, er... take this into the other room please?"

"Sure. Whatever you say, Master."

Heidi took the bowl and left, whereupon Father Geoffrey slipped into the kitchen.

"Hey, Tom. Everything alright?"

"Hey, Padre. Yes, everything is fine."

"The play is in good shape."

"Yes, I am very pleased with it."

"I looked into the dress rehearsal earlier," said Father Geoffrey.

"Oh yes?"

"Yes. I thought I detected certain resonances."

Tom stopped chopping, and turned to face him. Heidi came back from delivering the salad but, seeing the priest, hung back beyond the doorway.

"How do you mean 'resonances'?" asked Tom stiffly.

"You can't fool me, Tom. I see the way you are around Heidi. Are you sure you know what you're doing?"

"Geoffrey, I can't help myself."

"I know the feeling. Don't look so surprised, I wasn't always a priest, you know. She's a young woman. She probably wants marriage and children. Are you prepared for that?

Tom reflected on this for a second, examining his feelings for the umpteenth time. He sensed that, once he verbalized them to Father Geoffrey, he would have crossed a Rubicon from which there would be no turning back.

"Yes," he said simply.

Father Geoffrey genially put his hand on Tom's shoulder and patted him gently.

Heidi, sensing that Tom needed rescuing from some situation, bustled back into the kitchen. The priest beamed at her and retreated to the other room.

"You okay, Tom?"

"Sure."

"What did the good father want? It looked serious."

"A lecture in morality. Much needed, I think."

They each returned to preparing food. The curry was coming along well, but they both sneezed mightily when Tom nervously dropped the cayenne. Heidi stirred the pasta sauce, gradually adding more tomato puree.

The suspense increased. The noise level in the other room rendered their silence the more intense. Finally, Heidi blurted out, "Tom."

"Yes?"

"Would you mind driving me home after the party?"

"Mind?" said Tom, scarcely able to believe his ears. "Of course I will."

~

The area outside Heidi's place was deserted except for an idling taxi at the end of the street and a huge, orange cat performing a kind of tango as it warily encircled a discarded plastic bag. The few, weak street lamps cast weird specks of light onto the leaves of the trees which towered above them, and created watery, yellow pools on the sidewalks. Someone, somewhere was in their backyard, noisily putting out their garbage cans. The faint strains of a Roy Orbison record drifted from the upstairs window of a nearby house.

Tom watched Heidi crossing the street. At the bottom of the steps she paused briefly and turned to give him a wave. She unlocked the door, and went inside, but she could be seen on the other side of the glass for some minutes.

Tom knew she was looking out at him, and he thought he saw her blow a kiss.

There had been a moment, just before she got out of the car, when, had he pressed it, he was certain a kiss would have taken place: but against his will he kept to Blaine's advice. Then just as she backed out of the vehicle, she had reached over and touched his cheek.

~

Normally, Leslie would have been in bed at this hour, but had been kept awake by her sixth sense. She had been reading and her magazines were strewn all over the couch.

She stood at the window as Heidi came in and cleared a space to sit down. "You didn't walk home?"

"No."

"And there are no buses at this time of night."

"No."

"So, who drove you?"

"Tom."

"Who's that?"

"The director."

"The politician?"

"Yes, that's him."

"The old guy?"

"He's not so old."

"You were out in the car for quite a while."

Heidi tossed her bag on the floor and kicked off her shoes.

"You're holding out on me. I can tell." Leslie sounded piqued.

"Okay, okay. If you must know, I think he's interested in me."

"'Interested'," mocked Leslie. "What the hell does that mean?"

"I'm not sure."

"It means he wants your body! That's what it means."

"No, more than that. I think he really likes me."

"He's about the same age as your father isn't he?" Leslie insisted.

"No!" Heidi exclaimed. "Dad's a lot older. Is this cross examination over?"

"Stay away from him, Heidi. He's an old man, for Christ's sake!"

"Goodnight, Leslie," Heidi said curtly, going into her room and slamming the door.

15

Before Tom went in to work the next morning, he made a quick call to Blaine. He felt he needed to relate what had happened the previous evening, and wanted to receive confirmation that things were going his way and that he was on the right track.

Blaine made him tell the entire story from the theatre to the party and the drive home.

"She touched your cheek?"

"Yes."

"What kind of a touch was it?"

"How do you mean?"

"Was it an accident? Was she punching you in the face? Was it just a brush, or was it tender and lingering?"

"You are such an ass, Blaine," said Tom. "Of course it was tender and lingering. Otherwise I wouldn't have mentioned it."

"Well, I had to be sure before I could analyze the current position."

"And what is your analysis, O Great Guru?"

"I think it is safe to say that the touch on the cheek means something. The question is what. It could have been a sisterly gesture of affection to thank you for driving her home, or it might, I say might, have meant she has feelings for you, but was not sufficiently convinced about them to do anything more than touch."

"What are the odds now? Do you think they are narrowing?"

"I'd say we are down to sixty/forty, but still against."

"Still against?"

"Better to be prepared to face the discovery that this was all wishful thinking," said Blaine sagely. "Human beings have an infinite capacity to talk themselves into believing that what they want is real, as opposed to being fantasy."

"I take your point," said Tom. "Thanks, pal."

"Don't mention it. My bill is in the mail."

~

Once in his office, Tom called Wendell to see if he would be free for coffee or lunch. Wendell's secretary told him her minister was tied up for lunch, but she would ask Wendell to get back to him about coffee.

Within ten minutes the phone rang.

"What's up, buddy?" It was Wendell's booming baritone voice.

"Hey, Wendell. You mentioned the other day that you wanted a chat. I wondered if you could get away some time later today."

"Let me take a look at my diary. Er...let's see...yeah, I can manage a half hour at eleven."

"Good. Where?"

"Meet you at the cafeteria in the Art Gallery."

"You're on. See you then."

Tom busied himself with some correspondence.

A few minutes later, Stephanie put her head around the door. "Hey, Tom. What're you doing for coffee?"

"Oh, hey, Steph. I just this minute arranged to meet Wendell."

"Mind if I tag along?"

"I wouldn't mind Stephanie, but I kind of got the impression that Wendell wanted to discuss something personal."

"Okay. Another time. Toodles, Tom."

"Toodles, Stephanie."

Tom arrived at the cafeteria first, got himself a coffee and found a table by the window. He idly gazed out, noticing how quickly the summer was advancing. The evenings were no longer chilly and daytime temperatures were climbing. He was hoping for a particularly fine summer because he devoutly hoped he might be sharing it with Heidi.

His reverie was interrupted by Wendell looming over him and plonking a coffee down on the table.

"Who's been a naughty boy, then?" Wendell said without any introductory niceties.

"What are you talking about?"

"I'm hearing rumours. Nothing substantial yet, just a few whispers, about you having the hots for some young thing. Anything in it?"

"Yes, if you must know," said Tom, lowering his voice, "but that's all it is. I haven't acted on it."

"But you will." Wendell chuckled.

"I don't know. It's possible, It's early days yet."

"Anyone I know?"

"Yes. You must keep this to yourself."

"You have my word."

"It's Heidi Granger," said Tom, dropping his voice to a whisper.

"Who's that?" Wendell asked. Then, realizing, his eyes opened wide and his jaw dropped. "You're kidding? Tell me you're joking."

"I'm not."

"Well, buddy, you've got yourself a situation. I have no idea how the Boss would take this if he knew, but I don't imagine he'd be too happy. She's some kind of teenager isn't she?"

"No! That's the twins you're thinking of. Heidi's the older one."

"Ah. Even so."

"Any advice?"

"Hell no. I've got enough problems of my own."

"Not with Cynthia?'

"There's nothing wrong between Cynthia and me. We're a hundred percent."

"Then what?"

"The problem is my ever loving family, especially my sister, Grace."

"In what way?" Tom pressed him.

"In case you haven't noticed, Cynthia happens to be white."

"So, what of it?"

"Well, my family is unquestionably of the black persuasion."

"You don't mean they're—"

"Prejudiced? Hell no! You know black folks can't be prejudiced. They just don't think Cynthia is 'suitable'."

"But a nice black girl would be 'suitable'?"

"Bingo! You got it. Grace has got my mother and the rest of the family terrorized into supporting her opposition to Cynthia."

"No offence intended, but your sister Grace is...."

"Is one mouthy cow." Wendell finished the sentence for him.

"I wasn't going to say that."

"Oh, yes you were. Or something similar. And no offence is taken, I assure you."

"Well, yes, I guess I was," Tom said. "But her husband seems like a really great guy. And sensible, too. Is there any way you could work on him?"

"Matthew? He's an okay guy, but Grace definitely wears the pants in that family. Still, it's a thought. Maybe I'll take him out for a few beers if I can ever pry him away from the Gorgon."

"Good luck with that. And remember what I said about keeping that person's identity to yourself."

"Will do. I have to go. A lunch meeting of senior departmental officials. Boredom and dry sandwiches."

~

Although the food was only passable, the wine list derisory, the décor lamentable, the chairs hard on the posterior, and the tables tiny, Zack's was the "in" place for Halifax's under-thirty crowd, especially for those who worked in the downtown area. This was where Heidi and her friends habitually had lunch, and it was here she had chosen to meet Andrew when he called asking for a date. Young as she was, in Andrew's company she seemed years older and infinitely more mature.

"It was a real surprise hearing from you," said Heidi. She sipped a glass of cheap Italian white wine. "I didn't think you would have remembered me."

"No chance! Who wouldn't remember you?"

"You know," said Heidi, giving him a big smile, "you look just like your father when you give compliments."

"Let's not talk about him," Andrew said rapidly.

"Why not? He's a very nice man."

"He's alright for his age, I guess."

Heidi smiled again in a rather satisfied, slightly patronizing way, which disconcerted Andrew, who rapidly changed the subject.

"We'd better get going if we don't want to miss the beginning of the movie."

When they gathered up their belongings and headed out into the night, Heidi was still smiling, and Andrew was still frowning.

16

When Tom and Iris had first moved to the Halifax area, they be-friended their next door neighbour, an elderly woman who had just lost her husband to cancer. Her name was Chedva Bensaid, who told them she was Jewish. She explained at great length that she was orthodox and regularly attended Beth Israel synagogue on Oxford Street.

When Tom, in his utter ignorance, asked why she did not go to the Shaar Shalom shul, which was some blocks closer to where she lived, Chedva recoiled with alarm.

"Conservative!" She frowned and shook her head violently. "In that one, I wouldn't set foot!"

Over time she became a particular friend, often dropping by un-announced with a loaf of *challah*, a pot of *matzoh* ball soup, a dish of *kugel*, or delicious brisket. In each case, Chedva pretended she had mistakenly made too much of the dish in question and said they would be doing her a great favour, or *mitzvah*, if they would take it. They gladly did, especially as Iris was noted for neither her enthusiasm nor her accomplishments in the kitchen.

When Iris was killed, Chedva was an invaluable help to Tom and little Andrew, and they came to look upon her as a grandmother. She insisted that Tom call her *Bubbe* and Andrew call her *Alte Bubbe*.

When Andrew had gone back to Annie Mae in Sydney Mines, Chedva cried as if he were one of her own family, and thereafter had kept a close eye on Tom and his career. When Andrew returned to Halifax as a young man, Chedva, now in her nineties, welcomed him back with undisguised joy.

Since then it had become a tradition for Tom and Andrew to go to Chedva's house for Sunday dinner, something she never tired of saying was fine because she had seen "the three stars in the sky" the previous night. To these meals Chedva's daughter, Sarah, would also come.

An only child, Sarah, who was a few years older than Tom, doted on her mother but, strangely, and somewhat embarrassingly for the Aldridges, Chedva showed to her daughter noticeably less affection than she did to Tom and Andrew.

Chedva's house was a charmless bungalow in the suburbs on which little of her personality had impressed itself. Surprisingly, she had kept few mementos of her married life and none of the furniture, everything being modern and sterile. Her lone indulgences were Scotch whisky and a television, and the only adornments she allowed herself were a single photograph of each of Aziel, Sarah, and Andrew, and a holiday snapshot of Tom with his former wife. She held court from a large arm chair from which could see the television, which she kept on continually, although with the sound turned so low it was virtually inaudible.

Since Tom's play was opening in two days, they had held their last rehearsal that afternoon. It was what Tom called an "Italian" rehearsal, which the actors hated, but which he insisted must take place. This involved having the actors say their lines at double speed, the notion being that it would tighten up the cues and help prevent anyone—in Tom's words—of "making a meal of their role."

He was the last to arrive at Chedva's house. "I'm sorry I'm late Bubbe," he said, "but I was supposed to pick up Andrew at his place. But when I got there the bird had already flown."

"Yeah, sorry 'bout that," said Andrew, not sounding at all sorry, and shooting Tom a defiant smirk. "It slipped my mind. I was in this part of town anyway, so I thought I'd come straight here."

"Well, at least it shows some initiative," said Sarah. "He shouldn't rely on his daddy for everything."

"He has a phone. He might have called so I wouldn't make a wasted journey," Tom complained.

"Enough of this *broyges*," Chedva cut in. "I'm sure you are both getting hungry. Sarah and I will go and get dinner ready."

Sarah, who wanted to adjudicate the argument between father and son, settled herself into the Chesterfield.

"Sarah!" Chedva called in a surprisingly loud voice for such a tiny woman. "Come. Now!"

Sarah reluctantly obeyed the command and followed her mother into the kitchen.

Andrew sipped at the glass of the Scotch which Chedva had given him. She kept only the best single malt Scotch because it was always kosher, having only barley, water and yeast in its composition. This one was a 15-year-old Dalmore, rich and smooth on the palate and dark amber in hue. Andrew rolled it around his tongue.

"So, pops," he said with another smirk, "how's the great romance coming along?"

"Oh, drop it, Andrew," said Tom, "It really isn't any of your business."

"I'm just curious about the progress you're making."

"Well, if you must know, it's stalled, but hopeful. What's it to you, anyway?"

"Oh nothing, I guess. It's just that I had supper with Heidi last night."

"You did what?"

"And then we went to a show. A good time was had by all."

"You treacherous little snake!"

"Hey, it's every man for himself. You'd better make your move soon. If you think you're up to it."

"*Shlum! Trus!*" barked Chedva as she came into the room. "'What is all this argy-bargy in my house?"

"Sorry, Bubbe," said Tom, turning away to the window. The shadows were already starting to lengthen.

"We have roast chicken—you like that, Andrew—with *latkes* and *tzimme,*" said Chedva. "Now sit down at the table before I take the wooden spoon to both of you."

Sarah came in laden with dishes, which she arranged around the table. "The boys fighting again, Mom?"

"Yes. I don't know what about and I don't want to know. It's a good thing we are not living in the olden times. The *Tanakh* says a rebellious boy is to be put to death by stoning."

17

Outside St. Michael's church hall a large sign read:

St. Michael's Players
Jean Anouilh's *The Rehearsal*
OPENING NIGHT

The church parking lot was full to capacity, and light poured from the windows of the hall revealing a variety of vehicles from a Vespa motor scooter and a farm tractor to the premier's big, black limousine.

Not considering himself a man of culture, Parsons stood waiting by the car, quietly chain smoking. He stiffened when an obviously drunk homeless man staggered up the street and made for the door. Alert, Parsons was ready to head him off and redirect him, but the man, hearing the buzz of conversation from inside, decided to shuffle on down the street.

Inside, in pride of place in the front row were Brenton Granger, his wife, Florence, and the twins, Poppy and Petra. In the next row sat Wendell, Cynthia, Andrew and Chedva Bensaid, whom Wendell had brought to the theatre in his big Buick. Not far from them sat Stephanie Gilmour, looking as smart and stylish as ever.

Standing at the back of the auditorium were a very nervous Tom and Father Geoffrey, both anxious in case something should go wrong. Soon, the auditorium went dark and the curtain went up.

In the parking lot, the light from the big windows suddenly became much dimmer and warmer, so Parsons, mildly curious, went to the door, eased it open, and peered in. Through the crack in the door, he saw what he regarded as grown people who had nothing better to do prancing around the stage in ridiculous costumes, spouting words in a language which he could barely understand.

Shrugging his shoulders, he returned to the limousine and lit another cigarette.

Tom was surprised and delighted that the performance proceeded with only a few hitches, and ones which the audience were not likely to have recognized as mistakes. A lighting cue was premature, momentarily leaving Leonard to say a few of his lines in total darkness, and Dorothy's entrance was a few seconds late. In the third act, Hugh gave a cue from the first act, thus threatening to precipitate the cast into repeating what they had already done an hour previously. Fortunately, Heidi spotted the error and calmly brought them back to the right place.

Overall it was a fine performance, thought Tom, and no-one was finer than Heidi. She had positively shimmered, exuding breathtaking beauty and absolute confidence in equal measure. It was Tom's conviction that even a professional actor could not have done better, and he was immensely proud of what they had done together to produce such an excellent result.

When the final curtain fell, except for Chedva who was rather frail on her feet, there was standing ovation, everyone applauding heartily. Loudest of all was Granger, who plastered a huge smile on his face and turned and waved to the audience as if the success of the production was all due to his efforts. He then dashed up the aisle to the entrance so he could shake hands with all the patrons as they left. Wendell, Cynthia and Stephanie gathered around Florence Granger and the twins, slowly escorting them out.

After exchanging a few pleasantries with Mrs. Granger and his legislative colleagues, Tom went backstage to congratulate his cast and crew. It was very dim in the cramped passage from the stage to the dressing rooms, the only light coming from the blue lamp which was clamped to the stage manager's desk, where Phemie was gathering up her papers.

Tom squeezed past her, putting an arm around her shoulders. "Well done. Good job, Phemie. Thanks for all your hard work."

"That's okay, Tom. It was my pleasure."

Just up ahead, a glimmer of light was sneaking under the women's dressing room door, from which Tom could hear the chatter of triumphant voices. He pushed open the door, and called out.

"Great show, gang! Terrific job, everyone!"

No sooner were the words out of his mouth than he froze in his tracks. In this messy, crowded space was Marge helping Ingrid out of her dress, several others in various stages of undress, and dead ahead of him was Heidi standing, facing him, in only her underwear. Tom was rooted to the spot, staring open-mouthed at Heidi.

Seeing this, Ingrid and Marge had a giggling fit, while a chorus of other women shouted at him."Get out Tom! Out! Out!"

Tom retreated in embarrassment, but was still unable to take his eyes off Heidi. "Er...Free drinks for everyone in the lobby," he stammered as backed out of the room.

By this time, the lobby was packed with people, their bodies touching, talking, laughing and drinking. The mood was cheerful and the sound of chatter was almost deafening. Tom, still thrown off balance by the incident in the changing room, made his way to the front door and took a deep breath of fresh air.

When Heidi, now fully dressed in her street clothes, came from the backstage area, she spotted Tom and fought her way through the throng to get to him. "Hi. What are you doing out here all alone?"

"Heidi. Wonderful performance," said Tom, not knowing where

to look. "I was getting some air."

"I guess you liked my underwear," she said with a big grin.

"Oh God, Heidi I'm so sorry. Please forgive me. I feel like such a fool."

"No need to be sorry. It was a good thing I wasn't wearing La Senza."

"La Senza?"

"It's a range of very brief, see-through pants and bras."

"God knows what I would have done if you had," Tom said, his face flushing anew.

They fell silent, just looking up into a blanket of stars and listening to nearby frogs, and an owl hooting some distance away.

"Are you going to drive me home tonight?" Heidi asked.

"If you want me to."

"I do want you to."

"Then it's agreed." Tom could feel his heart pounding.

"We both should circulate and socialize for a bit," said Heidi. "You know, I have to compare notes with the other cast members, and all that stuff."

"Yes, we should. Shall we say in an hour's time?"

"Sure, that would be fine."

It was one of the longest hours Tom had ever experienced in his life. He accepted congratulations and good wishes, shook hands and clapped backs, in something of a daze, only half aware of what he was doing and who the people were.

Finally, when he was being trapped in a corner by a 'serious' theatre goer who was tediously analyzing every aspect of the play, Heidi suddenly appeared at his side, pressing into him, so that he could feel her warmth. "Let's go," she said.

"Please excuse me, Dr. Hanniford. I must go now," Tom said to the critic, who seemed mightily offended at having his interview curtailed. "I promised to take our star home."

They bolted for the exit, and ran the length of the parking lot to Tom's car.

"Am I really a star?" asked Heidi when they were inside.

"As far as I'm concerned you are."

Heidi smiled, closed her eyes and sat back in her seat, feeling happy and accomplished.

Tom parked in the street across from Heidi's apartment and turned off the engine. Despite the lateness of the hour, there were still a few people about. A man was almost being dragged along by a black, Newfoundland dog, and a pair of lovers was sauntering along, hand in hand. They sat in silence for an agonizing five minutes.

"Heidi," Tom said, "there's something I have to say to you. I just can't put it off any longer."

"I guessed, I've suspected for quite a while. Andrew gave me another hint when I saw him the other night."

"That little twister! Trying to steal the woman his father is in love with!" Tom paused. "There, I've said it. I've finally said it."

"I think I already knew," Heidi said, with a knowing smile, "and don't worry about competition from that quarter. Andrew is a nice enough boy, but I much prefer his father."

She leaned over and gently kissed him on the lips. Tom could scarcely believe his great good fortune and softly kissed her back. Suddenly they were all over each other, kissing furiously and passionately. After a few minutes, they breathlessly separated.

"You must go," said Tom.

"Yes, I know," said Heidi.

They looked at each other, and plunged into another embrace.

After a few more minutes, Tom pulled away. "Darling, if you don't go now I can't predict what might happen."

"Me neither."

But again they started kissing, this time in a slow, deep, devoted way.

Eventually, Heidi broke away, her face brightly flushed and her hair dishevelled. "Oh God. I must go. I must!"

As she slid to the car door, Tom edged after her. They kissed again, and their mouths were connected even when Heidi was half way out onto the sidewalk.

"Goodnight, Tom," she said very quietly. "I'll see you tomorrow."

She hurried across the street, ran up the steps, turned at the top and blew him a kiss.

Tom Aldridge had never known such happiness.

18

After a number of false starts, summer had finally arrived, as was witnessed by the new, bright, yellow-green leaves which adorned the hundreds of trees lining Halifax's streets. It was now the third Wednesday in June, which all of Nova Scotia's social climbers knew was the date of the Lieutenant Governor's garden party. In theory, all nine hundred and seventy thousand Nova Scotians were invited to attend, but usually only several hundred actually went.

The present building was the initiative of Sir John Wentworth, the twelfth governor of the province, who strenuously objected to the accommodations provided for him when he arrived in Halifax in 1792. He described them as being constructed of green wood and rotting timbers, and said the entire edifice was in danger of falling into the cellar. A new, more fitting, residence had therefore been urgently required.

Even in those far-off days, inclusion was thought appropriate, Wentworth apparently insisting that the building materials for his new house be obtained from no fewer than twelve counties. In consequence, the present day visitor encountered an imposing, if not very imaginative, old building.

Those who did attend the garden party entered by the main entrance, where they joined a lengthy receiving line to be greeted by the Governor and his wife. Thereupon they went through the house to the garden at the rear, where they would partake of minute sandwiches and tea. Within living memory alcoholic drinks were available at the garden party, but some snooty do-gooders had the rules changed and, according to some, the life had gone out of the event.

It was said that the change was occasioned by several cabinet ministers getting hopelessly drunk and flirting with the Governor's wife in an outrageous fashion. Bad behaviour on the part of a Member of the Legislature was also responsible for the staff locking away the silverware on such occasions, following his stealing several spoons.

A large crowd had assembled, the ladies using the event to show off their hats, some of which were small and demure, most moderately conservative and a few rather more risqué. Zandili Joseph, always anxious to display her African roots (in actuality, her people had come from the Caribbean) sported an enormous Zulu basket hat in eight different bright colours.

The party had two focal points: The Lieutenant Governor and his wife; and the premier, his family and entourage. Indeed, it was difficult to determine which of the province's top two dignitaries had attracted the larger following but, generally speaking, the vice-regal couple had the older, quieter, non-political attendees, while Granger had the more boisterous, partisan adherents.

As usual, Brenton and Florence Granger were surrounded by their son, Anthony, Heidi, the twins Poppy and Petra, deputy premier Ernest Maddingly, party chairman Arthur Cramp, party treasurer Sam McNeil, Wendell, and Cynthia, Stephanie Gilmour, and various other MLAs. Apart from the crowds, leaning against the august walls of Government House and half hidden by a bush, was the ubiquitous Parsons, never taking his eyes off the premier.

When Wendell and Tom arrived, Heidi detached herself from the family and made her way toward them. Tom thought her lilting walk and a pale blue summer dress made her look divine, and he was suffused with tenderness and endearment.

"Hey, guys!" she said breezily. "Wendell, do you mind if I borrow Tom for a minute, please?"

"Hell, no. I need to have a word with Uncle Arthur anyway," said Wendell knowingly.

He half bowed to Heidi then made his way to where Arthur Cramp was trapped by a large group of doting, blue rinse old ladies. Over in the premier's family group, Anthony Granger, looking puzzled, stared over at Heidi and Tom.

"Quick," said Heidi, "come behind this tree before anyone sees us."

They retreated into the shrubbery. Tom caught his trousers on a bush and they both broke into laughter.

"What is it? You'll get us into trouble."

"I haven't stopped thinking about the other night."

"Me neither. It's all I can think about," said Tom. "What have you been thinking?"

"I'm still a bit confused, but I know I want to see you again. Soon."

"Come to dinner at my place tomorrow, after the show. You like lobster?"

"Love it, won't that be a bit late?"

"No, we'll both be hungry by then."

Suddenly, an agitated Anthony peered around the tree, bristling with self-righteousness. "Heidi, what's going on? Who is this man?"

"This is Tom Aldridge. You must know him. He's one of Dad's MLAs."

"What are you doing back here?"

"Tom is also the director of the play. I had a problem with some of the lines last night, so we've been going over them."

"Well, you'd better get back. Dad was asking where you were. Goodbye Mr. Aldridge."

Anthony stalked back to his family on the lawn.

"What a terrible liar you are!" Tom whispered. "Your lines are perfect. Just like the rest of you."

"I know," said Heidi. "You're a bad influence on me. I'll call you at your place after I get home from the theatre. I have to go back to my parents to meet some bigwig from Ottawa, so I'll ring you from there. Must go."

She pouted her lips at Tom, then skipped away.

~

They had another good performance of the play with a full house, so were pleased with themselves, but Heidi had to dash off immediately after the curtain so she and Tom had no opportunity to talk. A sandwich and a glass of Scotch by his side, Tom was waiting by the phone.

Heidi was true to her word. She phoned him from a landing halfway up the big staircase where there were two armchairs, a table and the telephone.

"Hey Tom." She spoke in an undertone. "I may not be able to talk for long because there are a lot of comings and goings here tonight. I don't really know all the details, but it's about the election, because Uncle Arthur is here. The guy from Ottawa is some kind of pollster."

"Okay, then I won't keep you, although I'd like to—forever."

"You say such lovely things."

"That's because you bring out the best in me. Can you get away tomorrow night after the show—for the lobster?"

"Just try and stop me," said Heidi. Seeing her father coming up the staircase, she lowered her voice to a whisper. "Dad's coming so I'd better go. See you tomorrow."

She had just hung up when her father passed her, giving her a quizzical look. At that moment the phone rang. She picked it up while Granger paused in his position.

"Hello. Just a second. He's right here. Dad, it's for you."

Granger retraced his steps, took the phone from her, waited for her to withdraw some distance, then put it to his ear. Heidi could not hear her father's entire conversation, but what she did hear puzzled and disturbed her.

"Why are you calling me here?" Granger was speaking in a hoarse whisper. "You know our agreement. You're putting me in an impossible position....I don't see how I could get my hands on that much. I just can't find it....Look, I've got people here for a meeting, I'll talk to you tomorrow....Yes, the usual place."

When Granger slowly put the phone down, Heidi could not help noticing that his face was filled with despair.

"You alright, Dad?" she called up to him.

"What? Oh, sure, I'm okay, sweetie."

As she made her way home, Heidi was riven by two emotions, the exhilaration she felt about her rendezvous with Tom the next night, and the concern she felt for her father as a result of what she had witnessed.

19

Tom's apartment already looked more lived-in, more comfortable, as he had rearranged the furniture, subdued the lighting and put some carnations in a vase on the coffee table.

Over dinner, Heidi described the telephone call her father had received and his reaction to it. "Of course, I couldn't hear what was said by whoever was at the other end, and only some of what Dad said, but it sounded serious. I've never ever heard him sound afraid before."

"'You put me in an impossible position.' Is that what he said?"

"Something like that. And then he said 'I can't find that much.' What do you suppose that could mean?"

"I don't know," said Tom. "It sounds like he was referring to money, but I guess it could mean something else just as well."

"I feel sure that whatever it is, it's tied up with the election, but I have no idea how. I know that the guy from Ottawa and Uncle Arthur were talking about the election earlier."

"It's just occurred to me," Tom interposed, "that it could be one of our candidates giving him a hard time about his campaign allocation. You know, threatening not to run unless he or she got a bigger subsidy from the provincial party."

"I never thought of that," said Heidi sounding relieved. "That makes a lot of sense."

"I'll keep my ears and eyes open. There may be some gossip which could explain it. If I hear anything, I'll let you know."

"Thanks, Tom."

"There's nothing we can do about it tonight. Shall we go and sit down?"

"Yes, let's."

They left the remnants of the lobster dinner and an empty wine bottle on the dining table, together with a flickering candle which cast warm, gently dancing shadows on the ceiling. Tom and Heidi moved to the couch, and put their half full glasses on the table in front of them.

It was clear that Heidi, who did not need any cosmetic assistance to look beautiful, had nonetheless gone to extraordinary lengths to make herself appear alluring. With a look which could have melted snow, she regarded Tom in a way which only he, still wearing emotional kid gloves, could misinterpret.

"Did you enjoy your dinner?" asked Tom.

"Yes, very much. Thank you."

"I'm glad I didn't screw it up. I'm not a bad cook, but I need more practice. Chedva said she would teach me to cook Jewish food, but we never got around to it."

"Tom."

"Yes?"

"There's only one thing I want right now."

"What's that? I'm afraid I don't have any dessert."

"I don't want dessert," said Heidi. "I want you to take me to bed."

Tom had to take a deep breath. He was amazed he had come this far with Heidi, but he knew it would be wrong to press his advantage this soon. Besides which, he did not just want a conquest whose attraction might disappear in a few weeks. He wanted her to love him the way he loved her, and he wanted it to last a very long time.

"That's a wonderful thing to say, Heidi, but I have to ask you if you are sure, or if you are still confused?"

"To be honest, I am still a bit confused. It's a lot to take on board. You know, the consequences could be very messy with my family, friends, and all. But I think I am falling in love with you."

"That's marvelous news," said Tom. "And when you are sure, when you're no longer confused, that's when we'll go to bed."

Heidi, who was not expecting anything like this, looked at Tom with a combination of amazement and appreciation. She threw herself into his arms, gently sobbing with joy. "Tom Aldridge, you are such a good man. Such a kind man."

"As I said, you bring out the best in me."

"I'm so glad I do," said Heidi very seriously. "And I promise you that as soon as I'm sure—one way or the other—I will let you know."

"Thank you. Now, it's very late. You'd better get out of here before I change my mind and attack you."

"Ooh, that's a nice idea. But you're right. I must go."

Heidi put on her shoes, grabbed her sweater and made for the door. Their goodnight kiss tonight was especially gentle and tender.

~

It was now very late, and Heidi expected to find her apartment in darkness when she got home. She was not at all pleased, therefore, to find Leslie still awake, sprawled out on the chesterfield and furiously smoking marijuana. Heidi loathed the smell of cannabis, and the stench in the room made her feel sick.

Leslie, who was frequently in a belligerent mood, became even more combative when she was doing weed, and she wasted no time in pouncing on Heidi even before she had sat down. "So, where have you been?"

"At the theatre. You know we're in the middle of the run."

"Till this time? You expect me to buy that?"

"I was with a friend."

"Now, don't give me a pack of lies tonight. I'm not in the mood to play games."

"What are you talking about Leslie?" Heidi was tired and desperately wanted to go to sleep.

"You've been with that politician guy, haven't you?"

"Yes, I have. Why, what's it to you?"

"Someone has to look out for your best interests,"said Leslie. "And at this time of night it doesn't take a genius to figure out what has been going on."

"And what might that be?"

"No doubt he has forced himself on you. You just better hope you don't get pregnant. That kind is only ever out for one thing!"

"Listen to me, you silly cow." Heidi was getting mad. "Nothing like that happened. If you must know I wanted to, but he wouldn't."

"What?"

"So how could he only 'be out for one thing' if he refused to go to bed with me?"

"Because it's some kind of trick. Maybe he didn't think you were serious."

"Leslie, you're crazy!" retorted Heidi. "I was serious. Believe me, I was very serious."

"I don't believe it."

"I don't care what you believe. And you better stop smoking that junk before you become psychotic, because you're halfway there already! Now I'm going to my room."

20

At lunchtime the next day, Tom picked up Andrew and they went to McDonald's to get hamburgers. They parked the car, and sprinted through the rain to the restaurant. This was seldom Tom's choice for eating out, but once in a while he enjoyed the grease of the burger and the texture of the fries. Andrew, he suspected, dined here rather more frequently.

While they were waiting in line for their food, Andrew was fidgeting expectantly. "Something's happened hasn't it? I can tell just by looking at you."

"Really? What do I look like?" asked Tom.

"Like the cat that just got the fucking canary. Spill the beans, old man."

"Watch your language. We're in public."

"Right. Wouldn't want to lose you any votes. So what's the score?"

"Heidi and I have reached an arrangement."

"Arrangement? What kind of an arrangement?"

They collected their meals and carried them to a window table. The rain was lashing down, reducing visibility to almost zero. People could be seen scurrying across the street and pressing themselves into doorways to avoid the downpour.

"She came over for supper after the show and, well, we have an understanding," said Tom.

"An understanding?"

"Yes. She's going to let me know if she's sure she loves me,"

"Wow! I got to hand it to you. You sure put on some speed when you get a challenge."

"It looks very promising for me, Andy, and she is very, very important to me. She is not all important to you, so I'd be really grateful if you didn't muddy the waters. At least not until I'm know where I stand."

"I hear you, Dad. I know where you're coming from, but it's too soon to be making any promises. It ain't over till it's over."

Suddenly, Tom had lost his appetite, pushed his half eaten burger away from him, turned and blankly stared out at the appalling weather. It matched his depressed mood, as he was coming to the realization that, despite the progress he had made, his chances with Heidi were probably still fairly slim. After all, he told himself, she was bright, young and extremely beautiful, so could have her pick of a thousand men, and what were the chances she would choose him?

~

Later that night the rain, which had been relentlessly attacking the city all day, had finally moved on, leaving the streets damp and glistening. A brisk wind was worrying a discarded newspaper along the sidewalk in front of the church hall, and a bedraggled dog was snuffling in the gutter.

The show had just ended, but Tom had come outside long before that. He knew the play like the back of his hand, and had seen the performance many times, but the real reason was that he could not bear to watch Heidi on stage while matters remained unsettled between them.

The last of the stragglers left the hall and soon the parking lot was empty except for vehicles belonging to the cast and crew.

Tom was leaning against a lamp post when Heidi eventually came out and impulsively he reached out and pulled her close to him. He was surprised when she did not pull back.

"I have something to tell you," Heidi said with a straight face.

"Okay."

"Do you want me to tell you now, or later?"

"Later?"

"Yes, at your place."

"You mean...?" Tom was overcome with expectation, but still fearing the worst.

"I've searched my heart and my soul, and considered all the ramifications..." Heidi started to smile.

"And?"

"Tom Aldridge, I'm now sure."

Tom was simultaneously incredulous and cautious. "About what?"

"About you. About us. I do love you, Tom."

Seized by euphoria, Tom picked her up, whirled her around in the air, put her down and then, very gently kissed her. They looked at each other for a second, then Heidi grabbed his arm and pulled. They broke into a run towards Tom's car.

Tom parked the car rather carelessly, and they ran across the street, stumbled up the steps, clutching and kissing the whole time. Heidi continued to nuzzle his neck while he searched for his key, and with his hand shaking tried to get it into the lock. Finally, Heidi took it from him and opened the door. They tumbled into the lobby, and in the elevator they melted into each other's arms.

The dark apartment, only weakly illuminated by the street lights outside the windows, was abruptly penetrated by a harsh burst of light from the corridor as the door burst open and Heidi and Tom almost fell into the room. Tom kicked the door shut and, their mouths still joined, they undulated into the living area.

As they stood in the middle of the room, Heidi undressed Tom while he gently held her face in his hands, softly kissing her lips, nose, ears, eyes, and forehead. When he was naked, Tom slowly peeled off Heidi's clothes as she smothered him with kisses. Soon their clothes lay in untidy heaps around the floor.

Heidi giggled. "Now you know I'm a natural blonde," she said, sounding profoundly happy.

It was warm and still outside, only a breath of wind was rustling the leaves of the trees, and a solitary sleek, lithe, young, black cat seemed to be the only creature stirring. The cat rubbed itself against a street lamp, then stood transfixed as it saw a bird apparently sleeping in a lower branch of the tree nearest to Tom's apartment.

As though in slow motion, the cat stalked to the base of the trunk, paused then leapt forward towards the bird. The animal was not fast enough and the bird clattered into the air and freedom. It landed on the window sill of Tom's bedroom. The cat stared up at the bird for several seconds then, concluding that it could not be reached, turned slowly and padded away into the shadows.

The bird shuffled on the sill turning its eyes towards the window and looked into the room. There was enough light from the street lamp to reveal Heidi and Tom making very tender love, feeling and kissing each other's fingertips. They whispered to each other as if they were the first to have discovered this kind of happiness.

"I have never loved anyone like this before," murmured Tom.

"I've never been loved like this before," Heidi purred. "You are the kindest, gentlest man I've ever known."

The dawn was gradually starting to lighten the sky as they lay delicately wrapped around each other.

"It's kind of like our play," said Tom. "An older man and a beautiful young woman. Tiger and Lucille."

"Hello there, Tiger," said Heidi, showing him a very contented smile.

21

The next day was bright, warm and sunny. Even had that not been the case, it still would have been a perfect day for Tom Aldridge, who had never known one like it, and could not remember when he had felt so cheerful, so buoyant. He was tired from the night's sensual exertions, but fatigued in the best possible way. It was a contented, deeply joyful sensibility.

Tired though he was, Tom almost danced down the stairs of his apartment building into the street and, nodding and smiling to total strangers, made his way to his office.

Seeing an elderly woman struggling to get on a bus, Tom helped her up and handed her bag to her. Even though he knew from previous experience that the incredibly ragged beggar on the corner was a complete con man, Tom dropped a handful of change into his battered hat. A street musician playing an Irish jig on a badly tuned fiddle received similar largesse, and the perpetually sour-faced woman in the newspaper kiosk earned a broad smile and a wink as he passed.

A bawling baby outside a dress shop was first silenced, then transformed into a giggling, bubble-blowing bundle by the faces and antics Tom performed for him. Seeing a flower stall further down the street, Tom suddenly stopped, wheeled around and bought an armful of blossoms before heading across the square.

Ahead, in the middle distance, was Province House, and next to it the caucus office building, their windows flashing in the sunlight.

~

The secretarial pool for the government caucus office was in a high-ceilinged room, flooded with light from overhead fluorescent installations. A number of women, and a few men, were busy at their desks when Tom entered. The hum of office equipment and the chatter of keyboards was augmented by surprised cries and laughter when Tom weaved between the desks, distributing flowers to all and sundry.

Attracted by the noise, the rather prim supervisor, Mrs. March, left her little cubbyhole to investigate as Tom reached her. She was taken aback when, bowing, he ceremoniously presented her with the remaining blossom, then disappeared into his office. There was a raucous round of applause from the assembled assistants and secretaries.

Tom was anxious to call Blaine and give him the glad news. He had wanted to phone much earlier, but knew Blaine would be sleeping and didn't want to disturb him. He stood at the window, looking out at the sunny, dewy gardens as he listened to the phone ring.

In New York, adorned in a striped, silk dressing gown over his pyjamas, an unshaven Blaine was adding sugar to his coffee when the telephone rang.

Tom did not stand on ceremony, but came directly to the point. "Blaine? I've got great news."

"Tom? Is that you?"

"Yes. Of course it's me."

"What's up? You don't usually call this early."

"It's happened. Everything is fine. Just wonderful. Perfect."

"I take it you're talking about you and Heidi?"

"Of course, I'm talking about Heidi and me."

"Ah-ha! When did this momentous event occur?"

"Last night. It was amazing, wonderful, absolutely fantastic."

"Excellent!" Blaine stirred his coffee and took it into the studio.

"And do you know what's even better?"

"I'm sure you're going to tell me."

"She loves me. She says she really loves me."

"Now, that is good news. I congratulate you and I rejoice in your success."

"Thanks."

"If there is a wedding somewhere in the future, I expect to be your best man."

"It's a deal."

~

About an hour later Tom was swinging along the corridor, whistling *If I Were a Rich Man*, when Stephanie Gilmour came out of one of the offices behind him. When she hailed him he stopped, turned around and slapped his rolled newspaper against his thigh.

"The one and only Stephanie Gilmour, as I live and breathe," Tom sang out. "How are you on this fine day, ma'am?"

Stephanie smiled curiously at the rather different person from the one she thought she knew, and was used to seeing around the office. "You okay, Tom?"

"Fine. I'm just fine, thank you Stephanie!"

"I can see that," said Stephanie, laughing. "What everybody wants to know is *why*. Whatever happened to that serious, ultra-responsible legislator we used to know? Why are you going around being nice to everybody?"

Just then, Wendell's steel tipped shoes could be heard clacking on the marble floor.

"I didn't realize it was so obvious," said Tom, pausing to consider. "Keep it to yourself, Steph. I know I can trust you. I'm in love."

"Oh!" Stephanie as if she had been poleaxed. "That's wonderful, Tom. I am so happy for you."

Swiftly, she turned and almost ran in the other direction, bumping into Wendell on her way.

Puzzled, Tom stared after her, as Wendell came up to him. "What's up with her?" he asked innocently.

"I don't know," said Wendell, "unless there have been any developments."

"Developments?"

"With you and Heidi."

"Well yes, there have been some sensational developments, since you ask."

"And did you tell Stephanie?"

"Not who she is, but yes, I told her."

"That would explain it, then. Lovers never have any compassion for the unloved."

"Oh, what have I done?"

"Stephanie has had the hots for you for ages."

"Really, I knew she liked me, but—"

"One man's meat is another man's poison," Wendell said enigmatically, shaking his head. "But I'm glad things are working out for you. How you're going to square this with the boss is another question entirely."

"You're right. Heidi and I will have to talk about that. But for the time being we're going to have to keep her identity under wraps."

"I hear you," said Wendell as he walked on up the corridor. The sound of his shoes could be heard long after he had turned the corner.

~

On their way to the theatre that night, Heidi and Tom swung by the

park, which was suffused with the setting sun, giving an almost un-
real, rosy light. A few people were about, mostly dog walkers, one
of whom was bent over scooping droppings into a plastic bag.

They walked along, not so much hand in hand but with their fingertips occasionally brushing.

"I think we should put it off as long as we can," said Heidi.
"Sooner or later it is bound to get out, I know. But for now, let's just
enjoy what we have."

"I agree," Tom said. "There'll be enough hassle when the cat is
out of the bag. But we must be more careful. Have you told anyone?"

"Yes, I had to. Leslie knows, and that means that Francine will
soon know, too. Have you told anyone?"

"Yes: Wendell, and my old friend, Blaine, in New York."

"Been boasting about your prowess with younger women?"
Heidi asked, laughing.

"Something like that," Tom said with a sheepish grin. "I wanted
the world to know about us."

"I understand. I feel the same way. Come here, you!"

She dragged him behind a clump of trees and kissed him. The
kiss, which turned into another and another, lasted far longer than
either of them intended. When they looked at the time, they saw it
was quite late, so they had to run all the way to the theatre.

22

Outside, the day was ferociously inhospitable, with the wind howling around the building and the rain thrashing against the window panes. The trees along the sidewalks were tossing wildly, and pieces of litter were being scattered like confetti. There was absolutely nobody on the streets, and if there were any creatures, they were well tucked away in holes, burrows and bushes.

Tom was lounging in his armchair, doing the crossword puzzle in the newspaper, in the margins of which he had doodled a number of happy faces. Heidi was in the kitchen, whipping mayonnaise in a large bowl and adding olive oil a little at a time. Beside her on the counter were the cracked shells of several eggs and a recipe book which she occasionally consulted.

She stopped beating, wiped her brow with her forearm and called through the open hatch to Tom. "God, this is hard work. Why can't we get it in a jar like everyone else?"

"Because it's much better this way," said Tom. "Freshly made mayonnaise is the real thing. You'll see."

"I sure hope you're right. If I've gone to all this work and it tastes just like the stuff from the store, I shall be really pissed off."

"Patience has many rewards," said Tom, thinking of how patience had rewarded him in his courtship of Heidi. "My mother used to say: *Patience is a virtue, Possess it if you can, Seldom in a woman, And never in a man.*"

"Your mother was a wise woman," said Heidi.

"Not really. She was almost illiterate. She came from a Newfoundland outport, where the school wasn't up to much. I think they had no more than a dozen kids of all grades and one teacher, an old dame."

"You never told me that about your mom. Was your dad from Newfoundland, too?"

"No, he was from Cape Breton. He was a coal miner."

"That's interesting," said Heidi. "He must have been a good man."

"I think he might have been until he got hurt. But then he pretty much drank himself to death."

"Oh. I am sorry. Tom, How awful."

"It can't be helped now," said Tom, changing the subject. "Can you help me with this one? It's a seven-letter word. Blank, O-L, four blanks. Mushroom without gills."

"Boletus."

"Good God, You're not just a pretty face, are you? I'm impressed. Let's see how you do with this one. Regally blind. Four letters and we don't know any of them."

"Legally?"

"Regally."

"Lear."

"Lear as in jet?"

"No, as in *King Lear.*" Heidi peered suspiciously at the bowl. "This has gone all funny. I think I've ruined the damn stuff."

Tom came into the kitchen as Heidi was about to pour the contents of the bowl into the garbage. "Wait! Don't throw it away. It's curdled, that's all. You must have added the oil too fast. You can rescue it. Let me show you. Grab another bowl."

Heidi watched attentively as Tom cracked another egg, separated the yolk into the second bowl and gently added small quantities of the curdled mixture.

"Just a tiny bit at a time. That's the secret."

"My man is a genius," Heidi said, glowing with pride.

"I'm nearly as smart as you are. Now taste that," said Tom holding out a spoonful of the finished product.

"Wow! Amazing. It's almost as good as Kraft," said Heidi with a laugh.

"You little brat!"

Tom came round the counter and grabbed her, held her tightly and kissed her. They put the mayonnaise in the fridge for later, then went into the living room.

"Oh, I forgot to tell you," Tom said. "I broke the sad news to Andrew."

"Aww, poor Andrew. How did he take it?"

"It didn't take him long to adjust. After he sulked for a while, he said, 'Okay, Dad. It's cool. Go for it.' I think he had a problem seeing us together. You know, someone around his own age and his own father was a lot to accept. And there'll be others—many others—who'll have the same problem."

"I think we were made for each other," said Heidi solemnly.

"So do I, my darling."

"I'm glad."

"Can we live together? When we come out of the closet. After you break it to your parents?"

"If we lived together we'd never get any sleep," said Heidi with a big grin.

"But you will tell them?"

"Yes."

"When do you think you'll do it?"

"At the right time."

"When will the right time be?"

"I don't know. I have to pick the right time."

"I understand," Tom said, clearly unhappy. "Let's go and listen to some music."

"Oh yes! Put on the Bach one that sounds like a toilet."

"You're crazy as a bag of hammers."

"Put it on and you can hear it for yourself."

"Maniac," said Tom.

He went over to the shelves, took out Bach's second Brandenburg concerto and put the disk into the CD player. Then they lay on the floor, conducting the orchestra each with both hands and one foot.

Suddenly, Heidi sat up. "Wait for it! It's just coming. Here! There! What did I tell you? It sounds just like water going down a toilet bowl."

Tom grabbed a cushion from the couch and playfully pummelled Heidi with it. She rolled across the floor, laughing maniacally.

"You're insane!' Tom said, "Absolutely nuts! I'm in love with a complete lunatic."

"Isn't it great being in love with a lunatic?"

"It's wonderful!"

Heidi rolled back across to his arms. Then they very slowly, very gently, made love for the third time that day.

Jeremy Akerman

23

Until Premier Donald Cameron in the early 1990s, Nova Scotia's heads of government had their office on the ground floor in a cozy corner of Province House, the ancient structure where the Legislature has met for over two hundred years. At that time, the premier's office was moved across the street to the seventh floor of a concrete building which had been wedged in between two much older, more dignified edifices, and was given the postally-incorrect address of One Government Place. Indeed, judging by the entrance, one would not suppose anything of importance took place in this uninspiring structure.

When he moved in, seven years ago, Brenton Granger had not, as had most newly elected premiers, changed the furniture, put in expensive Indian carpets or had the Art Gallery install their finest paintings. Neither, for him, was the space to be littered with the trophies, cups, spades, trowels, helmets, flags and other bric-a-brac with which other premiers had been presented over the years. Nor were the walls covered with certificates of his university accomplishments, medical licenses, and honorary degrees awarded by colleges trying to get more funding. Apart from importing a few photos of Florence and his children, he left the office exactly as he found it.

For him, the office was not a place to relax or luxuriate; it was purely for routine business, and he spent only as much time there as was absolutely necessary.

Unlike his predecessors, Granger did not usually summon ministers and deputy ministers to this sanctum sanctorum; he went to them, frequently dropping in on them without notice, and often with dramatic results he could not have achieved otherwise.

Once, Granger had gone into the ill-named Department of Transportation, had snuck past the receptionist, and searched out a mid-level official to get certain information. On finding out that the premier was loose in his department, the Deputy Minister almost had a nervous breakdown, and babbled incoherently about channels and protocols.

"You know what you can do with your protocols?" Granger asked. When the Deputy shook his head in the negative, the premier lowered his voice and said, "Stick them where the sun doesn't shine."

As a senior surgeon, Granger had naturally encountered some bureaucracy, but not the multi-layered, delaying, pettifogging, obfuscating bureaucracy he found in the province's civil service, and he did not like it one little bit. On assuming office, he was told that if he wanted something, he should inform his Executive Assistant, who would then convey the request to the departmental minister and deputy, who would then instruct the relevant civil servant to respond back up the chain, all in the fullness of time.

For several weeks, Granger did it their way, then hit the roof, lashing out at his cabinet, telling them to make sure their departments understood just who was elected by the people and who was there to serve the elected masters.

A horrified ripple went through the government, with various Deputies warning that civilization would come to an end. Consequently, they devised different, more cunning ways to delay decisions and keep the cabinet in the dark.

But, one by one, Granger uncovered all of these ruses, and eventually told the deputies that he was setting up a special legal fund to fight any of them who sued for wrongful dismissal in the event they continued to defy him and, in his words, he had to "fire your asses."

Today, Granger was about to leave his office to mount a surprise assault on the Department of Education when his secretary, Mrs. Wilson, told him that Mr. Cramp urgently needed to see him.

Arthur Cramp, looking even more lined and harrowed than usual, was accompanied by Sam McNeil, who appeared terrified out of his wits.

Granger waved them into two hard chairs in front of his desk. "What's up, Art?"

"Brent, we got a problem," rasped Cramp.

"What kind of problem? And why is Sam here?"

"I had to let Sam in on it. You'll soon see why."

Granger's eyes narrowed and he looked at McNeil dubiously. He was not happy about the circle of those who knew about his difficulties being enlarged, even by one person.

"Alright, if you insist. But you better be right about this, Art."

"Don't worry, Brent, Sam's as good as gold. I trust him."

"Okay, that's good enough for me," said Granger. "No offence intended, Sam."

"None taken, premier, I assure you."

"Well, what is it?"

"You'll remember I told you we likely had enough money in the slush fund to take care of Madame X?"

"Yes."

"What I didn't know when I told you that was that, the day before, Sam transferred most of it to the Party's campaign fund under the names of several of our most trusted contributors."

"Shit! What does this mean?" Granger's face paled.

"We couldn't tell the donors what we wanted the money for and transfer it back," said McNeil, "and in any case I can't divert campaign funds without the whole executive knowing about it. And once an election is actually called, it would be illegal, anyway."

"Christ almighty!" Granger shouted. "What a fucking mess!"

"It's not Sam's fault, Brent," Cramp cut in. "If it's anyone's fault it's mine for not checking before I spoke to you."

"Alright, alright," the premier said impatiently, "but it's got to be found, unless you want to go into an election with a new leader!"

"That's unthinkable," said McNeil.

"Art? What do you think?"

"I've got to be honest, Brent. If it came to that, a win would be touch and go," said Cramp. "Personally, I'd say if there was an election after you had quit in disgrace, we would lose."

"I think you're right." said Granger. "Are there any special friends, friends with money, that is, you could go back to, asking for a special favour, without telling them what it is?"

"That's exactly what Sam and I are going to do right away. But I don't know how much we could raise. Would you say twenty thousand, Sam?"

"I don't know. Probably not that much. I would say five thousand is not a problem and ten is likely. Do we know...er...how much...er... Madame X is looking for?"

"Not yet. She's being coy. She wants me to suggest a figure, I guess, so she can say it isn't enough."

"Premier," McNeil spoke tentatively, "may I ask if...er...there are children involved?"

"No, you may not!" Granger was livid with rage.

"Sam!" Cramp barked at him.

"I'm very sorry, premier, but I was thinking that the more people, such as minors, are involved, the higher the price would be."

"Let's wait and see what Madame X's next move is. When we know more, we'll be in a better position to know what to do."

Cramp's voice had become like gravel.

"Yes," said Granger. "The problem is I don't know when I'll be apprised of the blackmailer's demands. And it isn't something I can rush. If I seem panicked, the price will go through the roof."

"Understood," said Cramp, rising from his chair. "Let's go, Sam."

When she saw them file out of the office and, again, when she went in to see her boss, Mrs. Wilson wondered what in the world had happened to effect such a change in these three different men, and what could have made them so miserably unhappy.

24

A heavy mist clung to the city and here, in the Public Gardens, it appeared to emanate in clouds from the small lake, and billow and spill out from the bushes and shrubs. Ducks which could not be seen, could be heard quietly quacking in the reeds by the pathway which ran around the lake. An incessant drizzle pricked the surface of the water, making the grass verges and gravel path glisten.

If any day were guaranteed to increase a person's depression, this would be the one. If any day could turn a good time into a bad one, this certainly had all the signs of being capable.

Inadequately dressed for the weather, Tom and Heidi sauntered purposelessly along, Tom kicking stones into the lake, and Heidi half-heartedly re-creating the hopscotch game she had played as a little girl. Neither of them had slept well, not for the usual, blissful reason, but because Heidi had been feeling slightly unwell for some time and Tom's impatience was, against his better judgment, getting the better of him. Just as he had known that he had to control his impulses during his courtship of Heidi, he knew now that he should do likewise with getting her to agree to make their relationship public.

"Let's go somewhere," Tom said. "Let's go to Zack's for a bowl of soup."

'We can't go there.'

"Why not?"

"You know why not."

"No I don't," he said. But he did know, and instantly regretted having said it.

"People know me there. The twins go there. Even Anthony goes there sometimes."

"Are we ever going to come out of the closet?"

"Tom, you're like a broken record. Give it a rest."

"How long do we have to wait? It's not an unreasonable question."

Ignoring him, Heidi continued to hopscotch along the path ahead of him.

Tom knew he had gone too far, but could not help himself going further, and hated himself for doing it. "Heidi. I'm talking to you."

"What?" she snarled, whirling round on him.

"I can't stand this skulking around. Talk about the love that dare not speak its name!"

"I've told you, Tom. I'll decide when it's the right time to tell my parents."

"And until then we have to keep it secret from almost everybody else. Can't you understand? I want to tell the whole world."

"Maybe you're just anxious to show off your new trophy. You want everybody to see you still have what it takes to get a young girl."

"Heidi!" Tom was shocked. "You don't mean that! You can't!"

"Maybe I do, maybe I don't. They are my parents and I shall decide when to tell them. It's my decision. Stop bugging me."

"Are you ashamed of me?" asked Tom, utterly miserable, the more so because he knew he was making matters worse. "Is that what this is all about?"

"No! I'll do it when I'm ready!"

Tom looked away across the lake, not knowing what to do or say, struggling to decide how he could relieve his pain. "Look, sweetheart, God knows I love you. I'd give my life for you, but I can't go on feeling like I'm some kind of criminal."

"Okay," Heidi said defiantly. "If that's the way you feel, why don't you go away?"

Tom stared at her for a second, torn between equally unsatisfactory alternatives. "Do you mean that?" he asked at last.

"Yes," Heidi said, slightly less defiantly.

"Alright," said Tom in the absolute depths of despair.

"Fine!" said Heidi and walked away up the path. She tried another little hopscotch, but it had no life in it and quickly petered out.

Tom wretchedly watched her go, then turned and disappeared into the mist.

~

When Tom got home, after wandering the streets for hours, he threw himself on the bed and cried like a baby. Later, he went to the phone, picked it up and dialed Heidi's number. When he heard Leslie's voice he hung up immediately.

~

At Heidi's place, Leslie hung up the phone. "Wrong number," she said.

"Are you staying in, or going out?" Heidi asked her, barely able to disguise her despondency.

"Going out. In fact, I'm late, so I must be off."

"Have a good time," said Heidi.

"Will do. See you later."

"Yeah. Later."

She heard Leslie stomp off down the stairs, then went to the phone and called Tom. When she heard the answering machine,

she hung up, then went to her room and buried her face in the pil-
low.

25

Matthew Downey lived in the house in which he was born, one of eight row houses on Maynard Street which had been built in 1878. At the time of his birth in the 1970s, there were many more houses like his on this street, and on the parallel Creighton Street. But the zeal for "urban renewal" in the years after Matthew's birth had changed both the street's appearance and its character.

When he was a boy, there were many more black people living there, and many more poor people, too. Subsequently, lawyers, doctors, and university professors had moved in and had "gentrified" the place with renovations and new structures.

The whole area was different from when he was growing up, and many of the landmarks of the neighbourhood's main thoroughfare, Gottingen Street, had been demolished. He remembered the large Metropolitan store and the Derby Tavern, which he frequently visited, and a fancy restaurant, the French Casino, which he never did. Then, there were two movie houses, the Vogue and the Casino; a bank; a large Sobey's grocery store; and a music centre. Matthew could even recall an expensive ladies' store, the New York Dress Shop, and remembered wondering how many of the local residents could ever afford to purchase any of its wares.

Wendell, himself, had grown up nearby, and often had seen Matthew around the neighbourhood. He was younger than Matthew, so they hadn't moved in the same circles, but he remembered him as a big, kindly figure who was good at basketball and baseball.

Wendell's parents now lived at the north end of Creighton Street.

Wendell parked his car close to the south end of the street, where he could just see Matthew's house but was unlikely to be seen by anyone who was leaving the house and then heading north. He waited for about ten minutes when, just as he anticipated, Grace came bustling out and hurried in the direction of the Nova Scotia Liquor Commission outlet on Agricola Street, where she worked as store manager.

He waited until she had turned left onto West Street, then hopped out of the car and walked up the street. When he knocked on the door, it was clear that Matthew was surprised to see him.

"Wendell! You've missed Grace. She only just left for work a few minutes ago."

"I know," said Wendell. "I watched her leave."

"Then why..." Matthew began, then stopped. "Uh-oh. I smell trouble."

"Let me in, Matt, I need to talk to you."

"Wendell, if you're intending to get me on Grace's wrong side, please take your troubles to another door. Seems I'm in her bad books even when I don't do nothing. I hate to think how she'd be if I really did something wrong."

"Please, Matt," said Wendell urgently. "This is important."

Matthew paused, hanging in the doorway and nervously looking up and down the street. He coughed, sniffed, then rubbed his hands on his sweatshirt. "Oh Lord!" He sighed loudly. "I guess you'd better come on in. Make it quick in case the neighbours see you."

Wendell followed Matthew into the living room, which was a spotlessly-clean space filled with many obviously treasured knick-knacks and elegant furniture. Matthew's bulk seemed quite out of place here, as indeed did Wendell's height, but they manoeuvred themselves between a bone-china-laden coffee table and a three-tiered porcelain cake tray, and squeezed into seats intended for more delicate beings than they.

"Okay, what is it, Wendell? I know this is just going to lead to pain for me. I should never have let you through the door."

"I'll come straight to the point, Matt," said Wendell. "Do you agree with Grace about Cynthia and me?"

"Oh no, not that. I can't be doing with that again, Wendell."

"Come on Matt, I've asked you a direct question. Now give me a direct answer."

"This for attribution, as they say, or off the record?"

"Alright, off the record."

"Hell, I got nothing against Cynthia whatsoever. Not in a thousand years. I only met her a few times and she seems right nice."

"I am so glad to hear you say that," said Wendell gratefully. "Do you know why Grace is so dead set against her?"

"Don't make me say it, Wendell. You know what it's all about."

"Race?"

Matthew glanced around the room, then slowly nodded.

"Doesn't she see how wrong that is? After all, she's the one always going around hollering about racism."

"Yeah," said Matthew, giving a knowing look, "but this is different. To her, this ain't racist because it's something she believes. And she figures if she believes it, it can't be racist."

"That's some double standard," Wendell said indignantly.

"But she thinks that black folks can't be racist because they been victims of racism."

"You don't agree with her?"

"Hell, no. But I been trying to figure out that sister of yours for fifteen years and I ain't come anywheres close to succeeding yet."

"Matt, I want you to try to convince her that she is committing a grave injustice in turning everyone against Cynthia."

"I don't know, Wendell." Matthew shook his head.

"For one thing, it would mean that after we are married—and we will be—there would never be any contact between us and the rest of the family."

"Yeah, I see that as inevitable. But what you're asking may be impossible."

"But you'll try? As a special favour to me?"

Matthew sat looking at him for several seconds before sighing heavily and hauling himself to his feet. "I can't guarantee anything, Wendell, but I'll give it my best shot."

"Thank you." Wendell took his brother-in-law's hand and shook it vigorously. "Thanks a million. I won't forget this."

~

As Wendell was leaving the Downeys' house, the premier's limousine was gliding along by Bedford Basin. Granger had agreed to cut a ribbon for the opening of an expansion to the community centre, and he thought he could just fit it in before rushing back for a special cabinet meeting to discuss the possible election.

As Parsons drove, he chewed his lip, wondering if he should speak. After about ten minutes of indecision, he finally broke the silence. "Boss."

"Yes, Reg," said Granger looking up from his laptop. "What is it?"

"I don't know if I should bring this up, or not..."

"Go ahead, Reg."

"I was wondering if we have made any progress on that problem."

"What problem?"

"You know the one. A certain female."

"Ah, Madame X?"

"Yeah. That problem."

"Unfortunately not."

"She laid out what she wants, yet?" Parsons asked gruffly.

"No, not yet. I can't make an offer until she does."

"Have we got the cash when the time comes?"

"That's another problem." Said Granger. "I thought we did have it, but somebody fucked up."

"Bastard!"

"So we don't know what she's going to ask for, and we don't know if we would have enough to cover it when she tells us."

"What are you going to do, Boss?"

"I just don't know, Reg." Granger said wearily, "I just don't know."

"Fucking bitch!"

"I should also say this, Reg, because it could affect you if it happened. There is the possibility I might have to step down and let somebody else lead the party."

"No way!" Parsons let out a howl like a wounded animal in a trap. "Fight the bastards, Boss, Fight all of the motherfuckers every inch of the way!"

"If I can, I will, Reg. But it won't be easy."

26

It was a grey, blustery day at New York's Kennedy Airport. Porters were clutching their caps, and discarded paper cups and brochures were being tossed about the sidewalks by a relentless wind. Outside Terminal 7, travellers were scurrying in all directions, and the vehicular traffic was barely moving. Blaine had to wait several minutes before he was able to pull out.

In the depths of despair, Tom had decided on the spur of the moment to get out of Halifax and go to New York. The House was not sitting and he did not have any committee meetings for the next three days. He knew he could entrust the play, which was heading into the last week of its run, to Madge, the stage manager, and in any case his work as director was done and his presence was no longer necessary. He just could not face another moment in town, seeing the familiar places where he and Heidi had been so happy.

"I'm honoured by the visit, Tom," Blaine said as he moved his car out into the long line of vehicles. "Even if it does take bad news to get you here, I'm glad to see you."

"I just had to get away. Just don't give me a hard time. I have had plenty of that from others."

"All right. But remember: if you ask me for my advice, I'll give it. No sugar coating. And there had better be more than one topic of conversation this weekend. I can only stand so much broken heart stuff, so please keep the snivelling to a minimum."

"I'll try," said Tom, a note of disappointment in his voice. He had been hoping for unrestricted understanding and boundless sympathy from his old friend.

~

At the same time, back in Halifax, Heidi was shuffling aimlessly around her apartment, going from room to room, staring out of the windows, picking up and discarding magazines. She had not gone to work, having called in sick. That was only a partial lie, she told herself, because she was suffering far worse than from any illness. Her eyes were bright red from crying and her nose was constantly running.

As expected, she had received no sympathy from Leslie, who sententiously said that Heidi had brought it on herself, and that it would work out for the best once she had forgotten all about "that old guy."

Heidi went over to the telephone and paused before dialing Tom's number. She got his answering machine again, so hung up without speaking.

~

Blaine, who had had his own share of disappointments over the years, was in no mood to encourage Tom's gloom by hanging around his studio apartment all evening. In any event, it was his firm belief that a fine dinner with fine wine was the best cure for most of life's setbacks. So he took Tom to Cyrano's on West 72nd Street, one of his favourite restaurants, where the staff knew him well and catered to his whims. They walked from Blaine's building on West 59th, as the wind had dropped and a warm sun had finally appeared, dappling the streets with shadows from the trees and holding out hope for the weekend.

Cyrano's was a secluded, discreet place which one might easily walk past without noticing. But once you were through the unremarkable front door, it became obvious that this was a restaurant for the rich and the influential, and indeed some of the famous.

The first thing Tom noticed was that, as if by magic, the noise of the city disappeared once the heavy door closed behind them. Then he became aware of the thickness of the luxurious carpet underfoot and the welcoming, dim pinkish light which suffused the room. So taken was he by the opulent surroundings that he was barely aware that an obsequious *maître d'* was speaking to him. He muttered something in reply and meekly followed Blaine to an alcove.

"Your usual table, Mr. Dixon," The *maître d'* half bowed to Blaine.

"Thank you, Gustave."

"Here are tonight's selections," said Gustave, handing them enormous, unwieldy, leather-bound menus. "Shall I send Robert over with the *carte des vins*?"

"Yes please, Gustave."

The *maître d'* glided away, shortly to be replaced by the wine waiter.

"Good evening, Mr. Dixon. It's nice to see you again."

"Good evening, Robert. I thought we might have a Chardonnay to sip on while we're deciding on our food. How is the 2009 Ridge holding up?"

"A wonderful vintage. The last time I tried it, it still had some vigour," said Robert, "but I feel it is at the top of the hill or slightly over."

"But you would recommend it?"

"I would, sir, because we have only three bottles left and this may be your last opportunity to taste it."

"Very well bring it, and..." he looked at Tom, "...are you thinking of meat or fish for your main course?"

"Er...meat, I think."

"Right. In that case, Robert, a bottle of Chateau Leoville las Cases. Do you still have the '95?"

"Yes sir, but less than a case left now."

"Excellent. Then we will have that with our main course."

"Certainly, Mr. Dixon."

The wine waiter noiselessly swept away as Tom and Blaine examined the menus.

"I thought the lobster ravioli to start," said Blaine. "That alright with you?"

"Sure."

"They do a very good rack of lamb here. I recommend it. Either that or the *poulet roti aux truffes.*"

"I'll have that if I may," said Tom, taking a quick look at the menu. "Wow! It costs a fortune. I'd better have the lamb."

"Nonsense! If you want the chicken, have the chicken!" Blaine said, taking the menus and placing them on a side table.

"Now. I've given some thought to your problem. The essential question to be answered is what do you want more: Heidi, or to feel virtuous and right?"

Tom stared at him for a second, and then rose. "I'll call her now. Is there a phone in the lobby?"

"I imagine they could find one for you," said Blaine with a patronizing smile. "They are fairly well equipped."

The *maître d'* showed Tom to a padded, sound-proof booth, where he dialed Heidi's number. There was no answer.

"That's unfortunate," said Blaine when Tom returned to the table. "But try to enjoy your dinner. Do you like the Ridge Chardonnay?"

"Very much. It's a lot richer than any other white wine I've had, and has a huge bouquet."

"That's partly due to the bottle age and, of course, the wine-maker, Paul Draper, who is something of a legend in California." Blaine solemnly sniffed his glass. "But wait till you taste the red. It will knock your socks off."

"I could use something to knock my socks off," Tom said ruefully.

Despite Blaine's best efforts, Tom's visit to New York was unsuccessful in dispelling his gloom and deep sense of loss. He was convinced he had lost Heidi forever, so the sights of the city did little to cheer him.

They spent some hours in Central Park, then wandered down to Washington Square. To Tom's bewilderment, they went to 21 Washington Place, where Blaine asked him which great man had been born there.

All Tom could see were tall buildings of New York University, and had no idea whom Blaine was talking about, or when this supposedly important event had taken place. He was singularly unimpressed to learn that Henry James was the mystery man.

"You're kidding."

"No indeed," said Blaine solemnly. "His house used to stand right over there."

"You like Henry James?"

"Ah yes. One of the greatest writers who ever lived."

"You can't be serious." Tom shook his head. "His work is tedious, and never delivers anything of any consequence."

"I very strongly disagree."

"His stuff is like a huge, glitzy Christmas present, but when you've taken off the ten layers of wrapping, you find there's only an apple in the box."

"You're entitled to your opinion," said Blaine huffily, striding off.

~

They spent the next day wandering around the city, and by the time they had walked back to Central Park West it was early evening, so they went to Jean Georges at Nougatine for dinner, where Blaine seemed to be just as well known to the staff as he was at Cyrano's.

They were early for their reservation, so they had a drink at the bar, where Blaine continued to try to persuade Tom of the merits of Henry James. To keep the peace, Tom conceded that James was an interesting and innovative writer, but not sufficiently exciting for his taste.

Tom had a warm shrimp salad as an appetizer, while Blaine had the caviar on toast. Blaine then had the veal chop Milanese and Tom the beef tenderloin. Blaine ordered Roederer Cristal 2004 to start and Chateau Pichon Longueville 2000 to go with the meat. Having looked at the menu, Tom was staggered by the prices a two star Michelin restaurant could charge, and once again thought that Blaine's business must be doing exceedingly well.

They ate in silence for most of the meal, not only because the food and drink were both beyond exquisite, but also because some of the affection seemed temporarily to have gone out of their relationship.

The next morning, Blaine drove Tom out to Kennedy and dropped him in front of the terminal.

"I know I've been a real pain in the ass," said Tom. "I'm really grateful for this weekend. You've been very generous to me."

"Think nothing of it." Blaine patted him on the shoulder. "I hope your lady comes back to you. If I were a praying man, I would pray for it."

27

The day after Tom returned from New York, the Legislature's Law Amendments Committee, of which he was a member, was scheduled to meet in an all-day session. Before he left the apartment he tried Heidi's number again, but her phone was switched off, so, with an even heavier heart than before, he set out for Province House.

When he arrived, various members of the legislature were milling about in the hallway outside the main chamber, in which the committee was to meet. As he came up the stairs, Tom noticed Brenton Granger, Arthur Cramp and Sam McNeil, just inside the Red Room, huddled in private conversation. Parsons was leaning against the wall just outside the open door, and it occurred to Tom that he would be able to overhear everything the others were saying. Dismissing it as none of his business, he proceeded into the chamber and took his seat.

~

"So I've finally got word from Madame X," said Granger.

"How much?" asked Cramp.

"Twenty-five thousand."

Sam McNeil whistled.

"Do we have it, Sam?"

"Nowhere close. The most I could raise from our special donors was just over nine thousand. They wanted to know what it was for, and all I could tell them was a 'special project'." McNeil was almost in tears. "All but one of them were saying 'come on, Sam, you can tell me', and of course I couldn't. Only old Barker forked out without a peep."

"God bless him," said Cramp. "Barker's as loyal as a dog."

"How much more do you think you can raise, Sam?" The premier asked.

"Maybe two, three at the most. How much can you lay your hands on yourself, premier?"

"Maybe four thousand. All my assets are tied up at least until the end of this quarter."

"I can find three thousand," said Cramp quickly.

"It still leaves us five thousand short. That's if I can raise another three, which is very doubtful." McNeil was apologetic. "You know my own circumstances, premier. After my business's bankruptcy, I couldn't raise enough for a one car parade."

"I know, Sam. You're doing enough as it is." Granger put his hand on McNeil's shoulder.

"Brent," said Cramp, "you're going to have to go back to her and say twenty is the limit."

"I don't imagine she'll believe me. She thinks I have free access to public funds!" Granger was bitter. "Still, I'll give it a try. Guys, thanks for everything."

~

The Law Amendments Committee meets to consider the fine details of proposed legislation and to hear public representations in favour of, or against, any particular government bill. Today, the meeting had been droning on for over an hour. At the central table, on either side of the Attorney General, who was presiding, sat government functionaries, books and files piled before them. On one side were witnesses there to give testimony, while on the chairwoman's right sat the committee members, Tom and Wendell being among those representing the government.

Listening with only one ear, Tom was idly doodling black clouds on a file cover. The witness had stated his case, but then insisted on repeating his arguments all over again.

Committee members were getting restless and squirming in their seats. In the row in front of Tom, Wendell scribbled a note and signalled to a page, who collected the note and brought it to Tom.

"Lift up thine eyes." – Psalm 121

Puzzled, Tom looked over at Wendell, shrugging his shoulders. Wendell surreptitiously pointed to the public gallery with his pen.

When he scanned the gallery, Tom immediately saw Heidi. She smiled and gave him a little wave. Overjoyed, he nodded towards the lobby, jumped up from his desk, bowed quickly to the chair, and left the chamber.

As he came through the swinging doors, Heidi was coming down the stairs. Tom pointed to the Legislative Library. She nodded.

The library at Nova Scotia's Province House is an extraordinary room, both because of its physical appearance and because it was the scene of the famous trial of Joseph Howe in 1835 on a charge of seditious libel. Historians say that his victory in that case established the fundamental basis for the freedom of the press in Canada. Puzzling to most visitors, however, is how the accused, the judge, the prosecutor, three clerks, twelve jurors and the general public had squeezed into such a small space.

The stacks of books extend from the floor to the high ceiling, and the topmost shelves are accessed by an antiquated wheeled ladder. Today, the place was almost deserted, the sole occupants being a lone student at one of the leather-topped tables and a buxom, red-haired assistant librarian seated at a side desk.

Tom nodded to her and went to the furthest corner of the library, feigning interest in a series of ancient tomes on the life of Robert Walpole.

Heidi entered and lingered by the periodicals table, reading the headlines in that day's *Chronicle Herald*. Out of the corner of her eye, she kept watch on the librarian, and when the woman left her desk to go into an inner room, she quickly snuck into the stacks and into Tom's arms.

Breathless, they were all over each other, voraciously devouring one kiss after the other.

"God, I have missed you so much," whispered Tom.

"Me too. I thought I would die, I was so miserable."

"Let's promise never to part again."

"Yes, yes. I promise."

"And we'll stay behind locked doors if that's what you want. I've got to have you, whatever the price!"

"Thank you, sweetheart. I hope it won't be for long."

"We'd better go before we're discovered. My place at six?"

"Nothing could keep me away."

They kissed again, but before they could separate the red-haired librarian came back from the inner room and saw them. The look she gave them was a combination of surprise and censure.

~

Since the theatre was dark on Mondays, Heidi had the whole evening and night to devote to her reconciliation with Tom. They sent out for Chinese food, ate some of it, ran off to the bedroom, then returned to finish the meal.

They talked very little, only to apologize again for having argued. They repeated their promise never to fall out again.

They went to bed before eight o'clock and went to sleep about midnight. It was the most wonderful evening either of them could ever remember.

28

Two days later, the morning was bright, with a brisk wind catching at pedestrians' clothing as they scurried to work.

Heidi was leaving her apartment for the bank when she was suddenly confronted by Trevor, her former boyfriend. He was wearing brightly-coloured, almost knee-length shorts, a Nôtre Dame T-shirt and down-at-heel sneakers.

"Heidi! Wait up!"

"Trevor! What do you want? I'm late for work."

"Be late, then. I need to talk to you. It can't wait."

"Trevor, I don't appreciate being hijacked like this on the street," Heidi said angrily.

"Look. I've heard you're seeing some old guy. I want you to know that it's not natural."

"Get out of my way, Trevor. It's none of your business."

"Our old friends know all about it. You're becoming a laughing-stock."

"Not as much as when I was with you! Now get lost, you creep!"

She pushed past him and stalked away down the street.

~

Early that evening, Tom called in to check on Chedva Bensaid because she had been complaining of a nasty cough. When he got there, Chedva was ensconced in her usual armchair, watching soundless television, and Sarah was on the chesterfield.

"Bubbe, how are you feeling?" Tom inquired solicitously.

"Not too bad, thank you, Tom. I'm a little better today."

"That's good. Can I get you anything?"

"Yes, dear. Please could you make the tea? You know where everything is, don't you?"

"Sure I do. Won't be long," said Tom as he walked into the kitchen.

"Sarah," Chedva said sharply. "Don't make trouble, now! I don't like it myself and, if it's true, it will all end in tears. But I'm going to keep my nose out of it, and I strongly advise you to do the same."

"Someone has to make him see sense, mother."

"You always were a *meshuggeneh*, Sarah. May Hashem forgive you if you turn my house into a circus."

Sarah tossed her head, jumped up and headed for the kitchen, where Tom was putting cups on a tray. "Momma's very upset about your latest liason." She curled her lip as if she were mentioning something grubby and odious.

Tom looked up, startled. He was not expecting this, and was unsure how to react. "My what?"

"Everybody's talking about it. Who is she? You didn't suppose you could keep it secret, did you?"

"I never wanted to keep it secret," said Tom with a sigh.

"Oh, that was the little slut's idea, was it?"

"Sarah, shut your mouth!" Tom was white with anger. "Why should it be any skin off your nose if I seize the chance for a little happiness?"

"Happiness!" Sarah snorted. "Is that what they call it? Some people would say it was only one step away from child molesting. It's disgusting."

Tom dropped the tray on to the table with a bang and made for the front door. "*Bubbe*, I'm leaving. Get Sarah to make your tea. And if she drinks any, I hope it chokes the dirty-minded, foul-mouthed bitch!"

The front door banged and, through the window, Chedva could see Tom storming across the road to his car. "Well, Sarah, that went well. I hope you're satisfied," she said acidly. "And forget the tea. I'll have a Scotch."

~

Across the city, at Zack's Restaurant, Heidi and Francine were having dinner at a window table. Heidi was struggling with a huge salad, while Francine was forking down French fries as if she had not eaten in a week.

A rap on the window pane revealed Leslie's presence on the other side. She waved to them, then entered and joined them at the table. "What's shaking, gang?"

"Not a hell of a lot," answered Francine, "We're just shooting the shit."

"Well, I've got lots of that," Leslie said with a laugh as she bunched up on Francine's side of the table.

The waitress arrived, and Leslie meticulously ordered her meal, asking for items not on the menu, and others to be removed from her plate. At length, she grinned across at Heidi. "So, how's Grandpa?"

Heidi looked up sharply and frowned.

"Oops! Me and my big mouth," said Leslie. "Sorry, sweetie."

Heidi's glare became stronger because she did not believe this could be an accident. The thought that Leslie would hurt her for sport filled her with disgust.

"What's all this about?" Francine asked.

The silence lasted for a full minute.

"Come on Heidi, spill the beans," insisted Francine.

"It's nothing."

"It doesn't sound like nothing. Who's Grandpa?"

"You may as well know, since Big Mouth here can't keep a secret." Heidi was bitter. "Or a promise."

"Well, excuse me," Leslie said, throwing up her hands.

"It's no big deal," said Heidi. "It's just that I'm seeing an older man. That's all."

"How much older?" Francine probed.

"Twenty years, is it, Heidi?" taunted Leslie.

"Thanks a bunch, Leslie. Yes, twenty. So what?"

"Jesus H. Christ," said Francine. "You must be sick. Eeeuw!"

Tears in her eyes, Heidi stared at her, smouldering with rage. Then she gathered up her things and walked out.

~

A few blocks away, at the Premier's Office, Brenton Granger was at his desk, carefully punching a calculator. Parsons sprawled in a chair, smoking a cigarette in clear violation of building regulations.

At length, Granger sighed heavily, and pushed the calculator away from him. "It's no good, Reg. I can't make it work."

"Is there anyone we can turn to, Boss?"

"We've approached just about everybody who has any money."

"I've got about eighteen hundred in the bank, Boss. You're welcome to it, if that's any good."

"My God, Reg." Granger was overcome with emotion. "That's all you have in the world. I couldn't take it, my dear friend, even if it would help. But we're very far from the figure we need."

"So, where does that leave us?"

"If Sam McNeil can't work a miracle in the next day or so, I'll have to step down. The party will have to go into the election with a new leader."

"Jesus Christ!" Parsons exploded, furiously hurling his chair across the office. "That motherfucking bastard!" He swept all the papers from the desk onto the floor, then pounded his fist against the wall.

Granger was startled, never having seen Parsons in such a rage before. He hastened to calm him down. "Take it easy, old friend. It may not come to that. Let's see what happens over the next few days."

Parsons collapsed to the floor. He was sobbing uncontrollably.

29

The next morning Tom was in his office, discussing some prospect-ive legislation with Stephanie. It was a hot day, so Tom had taken his jacket off and rolled up his shirtsleeves. Stephanie, who always looked cool, not to mention stylish, was wearing a white sleeveless dress and some very expensive jewellery.

They were trying to reconcile two bills dealing with the same subject, in order to produce one which bore the best features of both. This often happened when more than one government de-partment was involved, and each had been asked to submit draft legislation. Under most administrations, the Legislative Counsel's office would carry out this task, but Brenton Granger wanted products which not only satisfied the legal requirements, but translated the dry language of the lawyers into something which would appeal to the voters. This is why he insisted that the Whip's Office go over bills before they went to cabinet.

They had almost finished their work on the first two bills when the door crashed open and Zandili Joseph barged in.

"Tom, I gotta tell you something," Her voice was loud and hec-toring. "We've been through an awful pile of shit together and you helped me out a lot, but this stunt you're pulling now is making my stomach turn."

"Zandili, what are you talking about?"

"Shut up, Tom, and let me have my say. I don't know who she is, but the word on the street is that she's only a kid."

"Zandili, you can drop the moralizing tone with me," said Tom, seriously annoyed. "First, you don't know the facts and, second, you don't understand the situation."

"I sure can guess," said Zandili, parking her generous bottom on the edge of the desk, "You smooth-talked this innocent little girl and then you seduced her."

"What is this all about?" Stephanie inquired, clearly mystified.

"Lover boy has got some child hidden away somewheres."

Tom's face was now highly flushed, but his knuckles were white where they gripped the back of his chair. "You know shit all about it, Zandili. Now get the hell out of my office before I kick your fat ass!"

Zandili glowered at him, snorted, and charged out. Still fuming, Tom paced the office.

"Is this true, Tom?"

"Not the way she tells it, Steph. Are you going to chew me out, too?"

"No, Tom. I want you to be happy. I hope this—whatever it is—does it for you."

~

Later, Tom called Wendell and asked him to the Art Gallery café for lunch. With some difficulty, the latter negotiated his long legs under the table.

"So, the word is out?"

"It would certainly seem so. I'm not sure how it got around, but quite a number of people seem to know. They don't know who she is, but they do know I am a disgusting beast. Some of them, like Sarah and Zandili, are having a field day."

"Zandili? What's up her nose?"

"Defense of morality. Scourging the sinners. Sisters to the barricades. You know the kind of crap the sanctimonious cow can come out with when she thinks she's got a worthy cause."

"Brother, do I ever!"

"And now, I've got a message to go to see Uncle Arthur. There's not much which escapes his notice. Maybe Zandili squealed."

"Uncle Arthur will be fair to you," said Wendell. "Maybe stern, but fair."

"I hope so."

"Look, buddy, after you get through with him, why don't you and your sweet darling join Cynthia and me for drinks? Somewhere dark and discreet. We'll go to the Mombasa club."

"Sounds good. I'm sure Heidi would like to be among friends for a change. But it will have to be late, after the theatre closes."

~

Arthur Cramp had such seniority in the party that he could commandeer the Speaker's office at a moment's notice. It was larger than Tom's, in Province House and on the ground floor, with several large windows. Tom sat fidgeting while Cramp removed a bottle of whisky and two heavy crystal glasses from a cabinet.

"You'll join me in a little of the Speaker's Glenlivet?"

"Yes, please, Arthur."

"Did you know that this used to be my office? I was Speaker for eight years back in the Ice Age."

Cramp poured out two generous measures, gave one to Tom then carried his own to the window. "Tom, I've been in and out of this place for over fifty years. I've seen them come, and I've seen them go. I knew everything about them. All their little peccadilloes."

Tom stared at Cramp's back, wondering what was coming next. It might be that Cramp had a favour to ask. It would not be unusual for the Chief Whip to get such a request. Maybe this meeting had nothing at all to do with Heidi.

"Some liked 'em black, others white," Cramp continued. "Some liked whores, some liked boys. I don't judge. I never judged, Tom. All I ever care about is winning elections."

He walked back from the window and eased himself into the Speaker's padded leather chair. "The thing is, though, the premier is having some personal problems right now." He put his hand up. "Don't ask me what they are. I can't tell you. Suffice it to say that the shit could hit the fan and we don't need any additional manure flying around. Understand?"

Tom nodded as Cramp took a long pull at his Scotch. He put his glass down and, in silence, looked intently at Tom for several seconds. "I can see that you do understand. I'm concerned that the premier's supporters, his friends, don't do anything in the next little while which could add to his problems. I wouldn't ask anyone to put his life on hold, but maybe to cool it if they were doing anything which could cause complications."

"I understand," said Tom solemnly.

Cramp swirled his glass and nodded sagely.

~

The Mombasa Club was a few kilometres from Province House, in Wendell's constituency, and was only frequented by a significant white clientele at election time. The lighting was extremely dim. At one end a long, shiny bar, extending almost the full width of the room, overlooked a small dance floor. Next to that, a jazz quartet played what Chedva called "smoochy" music.

Most of the tables were discreetly sheltered by booths. At one of these Heidi, Tom and Wendell were nursing their drinks.

"How did it go with Uncle Arthur?" Wendell asked.

"You saw Uncle Arthur?" Heidi was surprised. "Why didn't you tell me?"

"I didn't want to worry you."

"Why should I be worried? What was it about?"

"He didn't come right out with it—you know how Uncle Arthur is—but he more or less let me know that it was about us."

"Us? You mean he knows?" Heidi sounded horrified.

"He danced all around the bushes, but the bottom line was that we should lie as low as possible."

"That's what I've been telling him, Wendell," said Heidi. "I'm not even sure we should be here tonight."

"Here's Cynthia," said Wendell.

They all stood up and Tom made the introductions.

"Hello Heidi," said Cynthia. "I understand we're pretty much in the same boat. Highly disapproved of!"

"I guess so."

"It's human nature. I don't exactly know what kind of grief you're getting, but I have an idea. You know Wendell's family hates me."

"That's a little strong, sweetheart. Besides, Matt likes you."

"Maybe," said Cynthia, "but the rest of them treat me as if I had leprosy."

Just then, a group of middle-aged black women wandered in from the foyer, laughing and chattering. Grace stepped forward from the group, and imperiously surveyed the room.

"Shit!" Wendell suddenly exclaimed.

"What is it?"

"Don't look now, but Grace has just come in with some friends. Damn! She must have come here after Bingo."

Like an Act of God, Grace materialized before them, and stood there with her hands on hips. "Well, hello there, little brother! And Tom, too. How cozy. The lovely Cynthia I already know, but I don't think I've met this young lady. I didn't know you had a daughter, Tom."

Heidi shrivelled, looking and feeling utterly miserable. Tom looked away and dropped his head. He was determined not to rise to the bait.

"Grace, if you're here to make trouble, please forget it," said Wendell. "We're trying to relax. Go back to your friends."

"Okay, okay. I'm not looking for trouble. Just trying to be sociable," said Grace superciliously, "I'll just leave you little love birds in peace. Y'all have a good time now, y'hear? Wendell, I'll see you at the house tomorrow."

They sat silent and dispirited as Grace strode back to her party.

30

If Wendell thought the next-day visit to his sister would prove efficacious in repairing their relationship, he was to be sadly mistaken. The first clue came on the doorstep when Matthew let him in.

"I'm still trying, Wendell. But it's an uphill battle."

"Thanks, Matt. I won't stay long if she's still in her high and mighty mood."

"That would be my advice," Matthew said. "There's been no change so far. I've been chipping away gradually, but it's like cutting granite with a butter knife."

They went inside, carefully avoiding the myriad ornaments. Grace's commodious figure was incongruously squeezed into a delicate armchair in the corner.

"I can't stay, Grace," said Wendell. "I just looked in to tell you that something has come up which I have to attend to at the department. It'll probably take the rest of the day."

"Suit yourself," Grace said with a sniff. "No doubt you'll find time for Cynthia, but not for your own family."

"Don't you ever let up?" Wendell sighed. "What happened to 'We shall overcome'? What happened to Dr. King's dream of a nation where people would be judged not by the colour of their skin, but by the content of their character?"

"That's not what this is about at all, Wendell. It's about you being headstrong, trying to be different, and looking down on your own kind. Ain't that right, Matt?"

"Don't be putting words into my mouth, Grace," Matthew growled.

"I love the woman," said Wendell with energy. "Can't you understand that?"

"Oh, sure. And you love her money, her social position and all her snooty white friends," spat Grace. "And speaking of snooty white friends, you can tell Tom Aldridge that he should be ashamed of himself, fooling around with that juvenile plaything. That's no way for a respectable man to be carrying on. Downright shameful, is what it is!"

"I'm out of here," said Wendell, moving to the door. "I'll see you around Matt."

~

St. Michael's Players' *The Rehearsal* had finally come to its closing night. The cast received long applause, Tom got a standing ovation and Father Jeffery was fulsomely thanked. He announced that the production had raised several thousand dollars for the church, and delivered a brief benediction.

Chattering loudly, the audience poured out into the streets, apparently satisfied that the tickets had been worth the price.

At the cast party following the performance, Heidi and Tom had agreed to keep their distance, but to try to sneak away early. This they did, Heidi ostensibly going to the washroom, but not returning. Sometime later, Tom surreptitiously edged towards the door, then quickly escaped into the night.

They had agreed to meet at a Chinese restaurant which was neither fashionable nor well lit, but stayed open late. Arriving first, Heidi ordered food they both liked: wonton soup, shrimp lo mein and egg fried rice.

Tom got there just before the heavens opened and rain came down in torrents, slashing against the windows and turning the street into a virtual lake of dazzling reflections. He shook his coat, hung it on a hat stand, rushed over to the table, kissed her and eagerly sat down.

"I am starved," he said. "I could eat a horse."

"There was no horse on the menu," Heidi said with a giggle. "So, I ordered our usual."

"That was another wonderful performance tonight, darling. You are as good as any professional."

"Thank you, kind sir. I wonder if we'll get to do another production together."

"Maybe. It depends on when your dad calls the election," said Tom thoughtfully. "Say, did you ever find out any more about that phone call you overheard?"

"No, not a word. Why do you ask?"

"It's just that, the other day, Uncle Arthur, mentioned something about your dad having personal problems."

"Dad? What kind of personal problems?"

"Art wouldn't say. He just said that I—that is we—should lie low so as not to create additional difficulties."

"That is worrying," said Heidi, "for several reasons."

"That's what I was thinking. Still it might be nothing."

"Let's hope."

The steaming food arrived, and they attacked it with healthy appetites, sometimes feeding each other, as lovers will.

Just down the street, clutching his coat around him, Anthony Granger was desperately trying to hail a taxi. After two cabs had failed to stop for him, he hastily took shelter in the restaurant doorway. When he peered through the rain-streaked window, his sister and Tom were huddled over their meal. He was about to go in, when he saw them stretch across the table and gently kiss.

Stunned, Anthony was uncertain what to do, but at that moment a cab came along, so he flagged it down and got in. His journey home was a troubled one.

~

Anthony Granger was not the only member of his family to be troubled that night. His father, sitting alone in his study with the lights off, was reviewing his entire life, and wondering what the future held for him.

Brenton Granger did not consider himself to be a bad man. Although he knew his adultery would be excused by many on the grounds that his wife had refused all intimacy after the twins had been born, he still knew it to be immoral. Had he been stronger, he would have rejected Madame X's advances, but she had importuned him at a time when his will was weakened by political misfortunes and too much alcohol.

Once in the relationship, he found he could not extricate himself. Although, until recently, she had never said in so many words that she would cause him difficulties if he left her, the unspoken threat had always been present, subtly indicated by gestures and innuendos. As the years went by, his visits to her became a habit which was much easier to continue than it was to contemplate ending.

Granger was aware that many of his words and actions in political life were less than sincere, but such behaviour seemed a prerequisite for success and, in any event, both his political friends and opponents were similarly guilty. After all, it was not as if smiling, laughing, waving and back-slapping were actively harmful acts, and stretching the truth to give people hope and expectations rather than pessimism could be seen as kindness.

With those two exceptions, Granger thought of himself as very much a moral man. He thought violence against women to be reprehensible, exploitation of children abominable, and cruelty against animals unspeakable. He strongly disapproved of slum landlords, companies that overcharged their customers, and those who deliberately misrepresented facts. He was not a religious man, but he subscribed, in theory if not always in practice, to the precepts of the Judeo-Christian ethic.

Moreover, Granger knew he had been a good premier who had not allowed corruption in his administrations, and had always attempted to legislate for the good of people in general rather than vested interests. More than once, he had admonished a minister for improper practice and when necessary had removed the person from the reaches of temptation. And he was proud to say that he had not tolerated civil servants who coasted along as though they had a right to a lifelong comfortable existence, rather than a unique opportunity to serve their province.

Most of all, in his own way, Brenton Granger was utterly devoted to his family and would go to extraordinary lengths to make them happy. Though he was physically unfaithful to his wife, Florence, he treated her with the utmost respect and insisted that others did likewise.

Most people knew very little about their premier as a man, thinking him a bluff, thick-skinned extrovert who was fazed by nothing, and who bounced back from setbacks with alacrity. They would have been surprised to learn that underneath that bonhomie and apparent resilience, Granger was a highly sensitive and easily bruised person, alert to personal slights and public criticism. Had they done so, they would have been as mystified as he was himself as to why he had gone into politics in the first place and, once in, why he had stayed.

He entered the political arena because it had appealed to his vanity. As a top surgeon he commanded respect and even affection, but the idea of being chosen by the people was something he could not resist. And later, he remained in political life, certainly because he wanted to get things done, but mostly because he did not want to disappoint others. He had a singular sense of loyalty, a quality he admired above most others, and while he expected people like Arthur Cramp, Sam McNeil, Wendell, Tom and Reg. Parsons to be loyal to him, he felt they deserved the same loyalty from him.

The prospect of his having to step down from the leadership was something he could personally bear, although his family would not treat it with equanimity; but he knew the effect on his friends and supporters would be devastating and severe. If it happened it would mean he would be letting them down, something he could not face.

With little hope of getting a good sleep, Granger went upstairs to bed.

31

The following day, two families were having their traditional Sunday meals. At neither event was the atmosphere conducive to the dissemination of the milk of human kindness.

At Chedva Bensaid's house, the occasion was conspicuous due to Tom's absence. For the first time in years, he had declined to attend, citing Sarah's unveiled hostility as his reason, an action which she in turn regarded as unreasonable.

"Just because I spoke my mind," she said indignantly. "Is no reason for him to go off in a huff, and then refuse to come to our Sunday meal."

"There is such a thing as speaking your mind," said Chedva, "and then there is acting like a *chaim yankel*. You could have framed your objections in a nicer way."

"Being too diplomatic doesn't get the point across. I wanted Tom to be in no doubt about the way I feel."

"You certainly did that, Sarah, and this is the unhappy result," said her mother ruefully.

"What do you think, Andrew? You must disapprove of your father's embarrassing behavior."

Andrew, who was quietly enjoying a glass of Chedva's 15-year-old Macallan whisky, would rather have been left out of the argument. At first, he had agreed with his father's critics, having initially had a similar reaction himself. But he was becoming tired of the almost identically worded litany from people whose motives seemed to be less than charitable.

"I would let it be, Sarah. It will work itself out one way or the other."

"Coward," Sarah said emphatically. "Come on. Tell us what you really think."

"If you insist, I will." Andrew took a deep breath. "I say, 'Good luck' to him. You should meet her. If you did, you would agree that she's a lovely person. I think you are carrying on like this because you are Dad's age and you don't have a man of any kind, let alone a much younger one. I'd say you were jealous."

"Enough!" Chedva commanded. "I forbid further discussion on this topic. *Farshteyt?* Now to the table! The meat will be ruined."

For very different reasons, both Sarah and Andrew were happy to obey, and took their places in silence. Chedva fetched the roast beef from the kitchen, then the vegetables and bread. She sat down and looked sternly at her guests.

"*Barukh ata Adonai Eloheinu melekh ha'olam shehakol niyah bidvaro.*" She said. "Let's eat!

~

Also gathered for Sunday dinner was the Granger family. Brenton was at the head of the table, Florence at its foot. Heidi and Petra were on one side, Anthony and Poppy on the other.

Though time and poor health had clearly taken its toll on Florence, she was alert, perceptive and very much in control in her own house. Brenton, on the other hand, was distracted and was drinking quite heavily. Anthony and twins ate heartily, having large second helpings, but the others essentially moved food around on their plates.

Sensing that all was not well, Florence decided that she would make the best of it. "This is so nice," she pronounced. "It's not often all of us are able to get together for a family meal."

Nobody responded. Brenton cleared his throat and poured himself another glass of Whitehaven New Zealand Pinot Noir.

"I must say, Heidi," Florence continued, "you're looking a little run down. I expect it was the strain of doing the play. Performing that big part several days a week must have taken it out of you. Did the run go off alright?"

"Yes, thanks, Mom. We had packed houses almost every night. We made thousands for the church."

"That's nice. For the life of me, I don't know how you can remember all those lines. It must be very hard work. Of course, I've always known you're the smart one of the family."

At this comment, Heidi blushed, Brenton smiled, Anthony frowned and the twins seemed unaware anything interesting had been said.

"It must be a useful thing for your social life," Florence said. "You must get to meet all kinds of new people."

"Yes, Mom. It is. I do. I have."

"Yes, Heidi." Anthony interposed. "I saw you with one of your new friends last night."

Heidi looked up sharply. Her mind was racing, alert for trouble. Where and when, she wondered, had her brother seen her?

Florence, who had noticed Heidi's reaction out of the corner of her eye, smiled. "That's nice," she said. "It's always good to have new friends."

"It was Tom Aldridge," Anthony persisted. "I saw you at Wong's."

The blood drained from Heidi's face. She sat on the edge of her seat, desperately trying to think of a way to move the conversation in a different direction.

"Tom Aldridge?" Florence asked, "Isn't he one of our members of the legislature, Brenton?"

"Yes. Tom's an excellent man," Breton replied. "He's my Chief

Whip. Very loyal. Does a good job."

"Yes, he seemed to be doing a very good job last night," said Anthony slyly.

"Wasn't he the director of your play, Heidi?" Florence asked very quickly, sensing something amiss.

"Yes, Mom," Heidi answered, glaring steadily at Anthony.

"Well, it's nice that you keep in touch now that the play is over. I'm sure you've learned a lot from him."

"I'll bet she has," said Anthony with a snort, "an awful lot. I'll bet she's learned all kinds of things from Tom Aldridge."

Not understanding his tone, Brenton and Florence frowned at Anthony. Heidi sat stock still, waiting for a further bombshell. The twins were looking at their phones. Silence prevailed for several seconds.

"Who wants more wine?" Brenton said finally. "This is good stuff."

"I've had enough wine, thanks Dad," said Anthony, choosing his words carefully. "I've had enough of everything."

"Whatever can you mean, Anthony?" Florence asked.

"Oh nothing, Mom," he said, keeping his eyes on Heidi. "It can wait until the time is right. Please excuse me now. I have to go to see some friends."

Heidi waited until she heard the front door slam before making her own excuse and slipping out of the house. She hoped to catch Anthony and try to swear him to silence, but there was no sign of him on the street. In an apprehensive state she ran all the way to Tom's place.

~

They lay in bed naked, as Heidi, with trepidation, related the events of the day.

"What do you think he'll do?" Tom asked. "I hadn't thought of Antony being spiteful, but then I don't really know him."

"It's not his nature to be spiteful, but for some reason he always has to put me down. He treats the twins as if they were mental giants and me as if I were a total dunce—"

"When, in fact, the reverse is true."

"I didn't say that," said Heidi with a laugh. "Let's just say that they are young and somewhat superficial."

"Okay. I'll settle for young and superficial. But what's Anthony's problem?"

"He resents me, but I have never been able to figure out why."

"It's because you're clever and beautiful, and perfect in every way."

"What a lovely man, you are," said Heidi, kissing him.

"The question is, will he spill the beans before you're ready? If so, it might be better for you to spill them yourself."

"I'll have to take that chance. I need more time."

"Well, the heat is on," Tom said seriously. "Virtually the world and his wife knows about us in the abstract. It can't be long before they know the details. When they do, all hell will break loose. Even the media may get involved."

"The media? Oh, Jesus!"

"It will depend upon what else is in the news. If it's bigger than us, there's a chance they'll lose us in the shuffle."

"Why can't they leave us alone? We're not doing anyone any harm. Being in love shouldn't feel like it's a crime!"

"It's not. Don't ever feel that."

They lay in silence for some time, staring at the ceiling. Tom reached out under the blankets to find Heidi's hand coming toward him. He gently stroked her fingers, then ran his hand up her arm. As soon as he touched her breast, she instantly moved into his embrace.

"Do you remember Tiger's lines in the play?" Tom asked some time later. "Where he says everyone is trying to drive them apart?"

"That they would conspire to commit a crime?"

"Yes, that's it. The crime of separating them. We mustn't let them do that to us. If they succeeded, it would be a crime."

"I wish we could just tell the world to fuck off," Heidi said vehemently.

"Let's do it. Now."

"Right now?" Heidi was grinning.

"Right now."

They leapt out of bed, ran to the window and opened it to its fullest extent. Then, leaning as far out as they could, they shouted into the night, "Fuck off, world!"

Across the street, a few yards up from the apartment, a homeless man was sitting on the ground, leaning against a tree. Hearing them shout, he looked up and saw a naked man and a breathtaking, beautifully-endowed woman hanging from a window.

He waved at them. "Fuck you, too!" he bellowed.

32

The following evening, the premier was in rare form. He attended a constituency meeting where he had them rolling in the aisles with his jokes, stomping on the floor over his attacks on his opponents, and up on their feet for his rousing peroration.

"Not as long as I have breath in my body," Granger said in ringing tones, "will I allow our beloved province to be turned over to a know-nothing, opportunistic fellow who has the brains of a flea and the courage of a mouse!"

How they roared! It had been a barn burner, a roof raiser. He still had it. He was, he thought, at the pinnacle of his powers with, maybe, his best years still ahead of him. He earnestly hoped he would be able to continue to put them to good use in the service of the people.

It was not that he thought the party lacked talent—there were maybe four or five members of the caucus who could succeed him as Leader—but he doubted anyone other than himself could guarantee a convincing win at the polls.

Granger knew that this was a precarious business, and that, as British Prime Minister Harold Wilson once said, a fortnight in politics was a long time. Winds which blew one way today, could easily blow in the other direction tomorrow. A series of polls conducted by the party, and his closest colleagues, were agreed that his reputation and record were sufficient to withstand the vagaries of public opinion to the extent that an election held within the next year would likely return his party to power with a comfortable majority. However, without him as its Leader, the odds on that re-election dropped considerably.

The burning question was when to go to the polls. Constitutionally, they could wait another nineteen months before the law required them to seek a fresh mandate. Granger had almost made up his mind that he would seek a dissolution sooner rather than later, maybe as early as October; but then the Madame X difficulty had raised its ugly head, and he had been forced to reconsider.

There was no way of knowing whether his popularity could withstand the publicity generated by revelations of an adulterous relationship, and especially if the spurned woman spiced the fanfare with false accusations of abuse and bizarre or perverted sexual practices. As Granger's biggest assets were that he was trusted by the electorate and was seen as a sound family man, both he and Arthur Cramp thought that such public disclosures would be irreparably damaging to him and to the party.

So enthusiastic was the crowd that supporters blocked the aisle, wanting to shake his hand, so it took Granger a good half hour before he got out to the car. Parsons was by the door, quietly smoking.

"Ready to go, boss?"

"Yes please, Reg."

"Home or office?"

"Office."

The limousine pulled out into traffic and gradually made its way to the downtown area. After a while, they were heading north up Water Street.

"I raised the rafters tonight, Reg. Had them hooting and hollering."

"You always do, boss. There's no-one like you. You'll slaughter them in the election."

"You're kind to say so, but that problem has not been resolved."

"It's okay, boss. Your worries are over."

"I wish it was that simple, Reg."

"No. It's settled."

"Settled? How? Did Sam find the money?"

"No, I took care of it."

"What do you mean, you took care of it?"

"None of the others could help you, so I did."

"You're talking in riddles, Reg."

"That woman won't bother you no more," said Parsons with great certainty. "She's gone."

A look of absolute horror came over Granger's face as it dawned on him what he was being told. "My God! What are you saying?"

"And the guy who was in it with her. I took care of him, too."

"You fool! You lunatic! How could you? Nobody asked you to do anything like that!"

"You didn't have to ask."

"Stop the car! You maniac! You monster!"

The car screeched to a halt and Granger tumbled out onto the street and staggered away into the dark. His mind was reeling. In a thousand years, he would not have thought such an outrageous thing possible.

This was worse than a scandal. It was a crime. Was he an accessory, somehow? Had he said anything, even hinted anything which might have given Parsons this unspeakable notion? And was there any way he could possibly atone for such a dastardly act?

Granger went into the nearest bar and headed for the darkest corner. Fortunately, the lighting was very dim so there was little chance he would be recognized, except possibly by the waiter, and he would know by the man's face if that had happened.

When he came to the table, it was clear the man was a new Canadian who barely spoke English. Granger ordered three double vodkas, and when they arrived he paid the waiter and downed two of them immediately. He sat there, his mind struggling to understand and deal with the situation.

What would Florence and his children think of him now? How could they cope with the knowledge that Parsons had killed for him? And not one person, but two? How would his cabinet colleagues and caucus members react to such devastating news? He could answer none of these questions.

He drank the remaining glass of vodka and stumbled out. The wind had risen and he lurched along the waterfront, going over and over in his mind this terrible, seemingly insoluble problem.

In his youth Brenton Granger had been an all-round athlete, proficient at hockey, baseball and especially football, in which he had excelled as a member of his university team. He had also done some boxing and a little wrestling in his time.

The one area of physical activity in which Brenton Granger was not proficient was swimming. He had never learned to swim. So when he caught his foot on a raised plank, staggered and fell into Halifax harbour he was helpless.

Within two minutes he had suffocated and within four, he was brain dead.

33

It was not until mid-morning that anyone one knew something was amiss. Granger had not returned by the time Florence, Antony and the twins went to bed, but they assumed he was working late at the office, something he did quite frequently. When he did not appear at breakfast, they thought he was sleeping in, and Parsons' not coming to the house to pick up the premier supported their assumption.

It was not until after ten that Florence looked in on his room and saw that the bed had not been slept in, that she suspected all was not well.

Calls to his office established that the premier was not there now, nor had he been in earlier that morning. She tried to contact Parsons and, being unsuccessful, telephoned the police at eleven o'clock. The two officers who came to the house learned from her that Granger had last been seen there early the previous evening. They told her it was likely a misunderstanding, but asked her for a recent photograph of her husband in the event it would be needed.

At Florence's suggestion, the police tracked down Parsons at his boarding house, where they found him asleep, with his switched-off phone by the bedside. When awakened, he told the police that about ten-thirty the previous evening, Granger had asked to be let out of the car on Water Street because he said it was a nice night and that he wanted to walk the few blocks to his office. Parsons said he then drove the car to Province House, parked it in its usual place, then had gone home.

At that point, the Halifax Police Chief, Walter O'Malley, decided that the case deserved serious and urgent attention, and assigned Inspector Armand LeBlanc and Detective Sergeant Laura MacIntosh to investigate. They started their work at the point where Parsons had told them Granger had left the car, and commenced visiting every commercial establishment along the waterfront. For some hours, they had no success because some bars were not yet open, and those which were did not yet have their night staff in place.

It was early evening before they found the right bar, and the waiter, a Filipino, recognized from Granger's photograph the man he had served the previous night. In halting English, he told them that the customer had consumed a lot of alcohol in a short time.

The officers left the bar and when, within minutes, they found themselves on the waterfront boardwalk, they deduced that Granger, in an inebriated state, might well have fallen into the harbour.

LeBlanc called Chief O'Malley, who immediately contacted the head of the Special Enforcement Unit, an integrated unit of HRP and RCMP officers which included the Port Investigation Unit. In conjunction with the coast guard, this group patrolled Halifax Harbour, Bedford Basin, and the Northwest Arm.

The following day, as soon as it was light, the unit, consisting of some twenty officers using jet skis and a Boston whaler, were dispatched. A little less than four hours later, they found Granger's corpse.

By that time, Chief O'Malley's attention had turned to a mysterious double murder in the city's west end, where a man walking his dog had discovered two bodies, a man and a woman, dumped in the bushes in Flinn Park.

The medical examiner told O'Malley the victims had been dead for at least three days.

When LeBlanc and McIntosh informed Florence of her husband's demise at ten-thirty that morning, and asked if she would accompany them to formally identify the body, she collapsed in shock and had to be taken upstairs to bed. Anthony, who had stayed home from his work, agreed to go with the officers instead and, at eleven-ten, he confirmed that the body was that of his father.

When he left the morgue, he went downtown to the bank where Heidi worked. After checking with the receptionist, Anthony was directed to the small office where Heidi worked as a loans officer.

Until her brother gave her the sad news, Heidi had had no idea that anything was wrong, not having been home for several days. She was devastated and wept inconsolably, but before leaving with Anthony, she asked for a few moments alone. Then she called Tom.

"Tom?"

"Hi, sweetheart. To what do I owe this unexpected pleasure?"

"Dad's dead."

"What?"

"He drowned in the harbour. They found him a few hours ago."

"Drowned? My God, Heidi, how?"

"We don't know."

"Where are you? I'm coming over."

"No you can't. I'm going to the house with Anthony. Apparently, Mom is in a state of shock. The twins put her to bed."

"Will you stay in touch?"

"Of course I will, my darling."

"Let me know if there is anything I can do to help. Anything."

"Just don't come to the house."

"I understand. Is this information confidential?"

"No. The whole world will know soon."

"Alright."

"I've got to go."

"Love you."

"Love you, too."

Tom sat stupefied for almost ten minutes, then he called first Wendell, then Stephanie, to tell them what he had learned. They could not believe the news, and neither could accept that Granger, normally the most self-controlled of people, could just wander off and fall into the harbour.

"That doesn't sound like the Chief at all," said Wendell. "Something's not right about this."

"Well, we don't have all the facts yet. When I get them, of course, I'll let you know."

"Uncle Arthur should be told if he doesn't know already."

"I'll take care of that. He was coming to see me anyway."

"Good. I'll call Maddingly. He'll have to go down to the Lieutenant Governor and get sworn in as the new premier."

"Maddingly? Jesus. Does it have to be him?"

"The province can't be without a premier. We couldn't arrange a caucus meeting in time, let alone a convention. He is the Deputy Premier, after all."

"Well, there'll have to be a leadership contest as soon as possible. We can't go into an election with Maddingly as leader."

"I agree with that!" Wendell said emphatically. "I'll get the wheels in motion."

"Okay. And, Wendell..."

"Yeah?"

"When the time comes, who do you think we should get?"

"Don't know. It's kind of hard to say. I imagine there are a number of our colleagues who will throw their hats into the ring."

"I guess so. But whoever gets into the race, I hope you and I will be on the same side."

"Well, there aren't too many in our caucus who we could both support with a willing heart."

"That's true."

"Okay. Keep me in the loop."

~

Stephanie was almost speechless when informed of the premier's death.

"I thought you should know as soon as possible," said Tom. "You were a great favourite with the Chief."

" He gave me my big chance when he promoted me to cabinet. I'll always be grateful for that."

"He was a wonderful leader, that's for sure."

"Tom. We'll have to move fast."

"I know. That's what Wendell said. We have to move fast."

Tom had known Arthur Cramp for almost ten years, and in that time he had come to think of him as a friend, but also as a crusty, hard, tough, unsentimental man. When Tom gave him the news, Cramp cried like a child.

"Brenton Granger was not only one of the best leaders we ever had, he was my best friend," Cramp said through his sobs. "It was me who brought him into politics. In a way, you could say he was my creation."

"It must be very hard for you."

"Tom, do you have anything to drink in the office? I sure could use a stiff one."

"Sorry, Arthur, I don't."

"Then I won't keep you. Anyway, thanks for telling me. How's Florence taking it?"

"Not well. Apparently she's taken to her bed."

"Then I won't call around there until tomorrow."

Cramp rose from his chair unsteadily. "You know what this

means? We gotta get our ducks in a row, and fast."

"Yes. Wendell and I agree with that."

"Wendell knows? Oh yes, I forgot you and him are best buddies. Look, I'll organize a meeting of the inner group, and we'll pick our man and get behind him."

"Or her," Tom said.

"Hmm?" Cramp looked puzzled and then slowly nodded. "Yes, Stephanie Gilmour. Or her."

~

Despite Heidi's strict instructions, Tom could not help wandering toward the Granger house that evening. He knew he couldn't go in, but he wanted to be near her.

There were two men in suits at the front door, but he didn't recognize them. Not political, he thought; probably family, maybe police. A squad car was parked across the driveway to the house with its lights flashing. Some curious bystanders were hanging around on the sidewalk.

Tom edged closer to the house, and when he was across the street from it, he ducked behind a large oak tree and he dialed Heidi's number.

"Sorry to bother you, sweetheart, but I've been sick with worry. I just had to hear your voice. How are you holding up?"

"Hello, tiger," said Heidi. "I'm not too bad, considering. Where are you?"

An inquisitive old woman had come up behind Tom and was staring at him, obviously eavesdropping. Tom stared back, and the woman quickly moved on.

"I'm right across the street. I know you said not to come, but I had to be close to you. I won't attempt to come in."

"Hold on a minute."

Seconds later Heidi appeared at one of the second-floor windows. Looking pale and immeasurably sad, she blew Tom a wistful kiss, then was gone.

Tom watched the window for another minute, then turned away toward his apartment.

34

The next day, the province's news media were consumed by Brenton Granger's death. Province House and police headquarters were swarming with reporters, and some national media and their camera crews had arrived in Halifax that morning. So-called "updates" were being broadcast hourly on local radio stations, interspersed with tributes from the former premier's political friends and enemies. The Prime Minister issued a moving statement, pointing to Granger's many achievements over the nearly eight years he had been in office, and to the cordial relations which had existed between them.

People in all walks of life were discussing the reports, each of them passing judgment on the dead premier's record and wondering if the public was being told the whole story.

Police Chief O'Malley assured the populace that the death was an apparent accident. He said that Granger had died from drowning, that there had been no marks on his corpse to indicate a struggle, that the Fatality Investigations Act would be fully complied with and that, while he would not prejudge events, he would not be surprised if the medical examiner or a judge ruled the matter death by misadventure.

Not everyone was convinced, especially those who had known Granger's habits and found it hard to comprehend his having drunk three double vodkas in a matter of minutes. Foul play by others was not suspected, but many opined that his last movements indicated he must have been under great stress and therefore might have committed suicide.

At Province House, and in the surrounding buildings, members of the legislature and their staff were in a turmoil of confusion and speculation. Everyone had their own set of facts and their own theories as to what had happened and why. In one office a pool was started to guess who would be the new leader of the governing party.

Accompanied by the Clerk of the Executive Council and a few friends, Ernest Maddingly walked conspicuously down Barrington Street to Government House, where he saw the Lieutenant Governor and took the oath of office as premier. He returned by the same route, waving heartily to the traffic, many of the occupants of which had no idea who he was.

Back at Province House, Maddingly remembered that he was supposed to be in mourning, and, while he made himself freely available to be photographed, he assumed a grave and sombre manner.

Word got around to Tom's office that Arthur Cramp had again commandeered the Speaker's office and was holding court, so Tom went over to clear up something which had been on his mind since their last meeting.

Cramp was sitting on the window ledge when Tom put his head around the door. "Come in, Tom. Take a seat."

"Good day, Arthur. The more you hear, the crazier it gets. Is there anything new?"

"Only that asshole out there. Just take a look out the window," said Cramp, pointing to where Maddingly was standing in the parking lot, surrounded by reporters. "If that doesn't make you sick, you have a stronger stomach than I do."

"I hope we'll be able to dislodge him when the time is right."

"Oh yeah. That'll be no trouble. Let him enjoy his fifteen minutes of fame. Imagine! He thinks he can fill Brenton Granger's shoes! Brent was the best premier I have seen in almost fifty years. And what's more, he knew how to get his party re-elected."

"Arthur," said Tom tentatively, "I remember something you said to me some time ago. You knew who I was seeing, didn't you?"

"Yeah, I did. I was surprised when I found out, but not surprised. She is a very beautiful girl."

"I thought so. You asked me to cool it with my relationship because you said the shit might hit the fan. What was all that about?"

"This is in confidence, you understand?"

"Sure. In confidence."

"Okay." Cramp moved to the desk, and sat down. "I'll tell you what I can, but be very, very careful what you repeat to that little girl of yours."

"I swear I won't tell her anything which could hurt her."

"Okay. Well, the shit did hit the fan. Between you and me, Brent was living a double life, and he was being blackmailed."

"A double life?"

"Yeah. Another wife, in effect."

"Jesus!"

"You think you know someone, then you find out you don't."

"And blackmailed? Who by?" Tom was incredulous.

"By the woman he was seeing on the side. Apparently, he had been seeing her for years. None of us knew about it until a few weeks ago, when he came to see if we could find the money to pay her off."

Cramp got up and went to the cabinet, where he poured himself a Scotch, downed it in one, then refilled his glass. "You want a drink?"

"No, thanks, Arthur. It's too early for me."

"Suit yourself. Anyway, Brent didn't have the money and, to my eternal regret, Sam McNeil and I couldn't raise it in time."

Tom whistled. They sat in silence for several minutes. "Arthur, is there any connection between this woman and the Chief's death?"

"I've thought about that, but I can't see a connection. I don't even have the slightest idea who this woman was. Unless Brent took his own life, it's a coincidence that these events have collided."

"What about suicide? You knew him better than all of us. Can you see him taking that route?"

"You never know what's inside someone else's mind, but I would say no, I can't. Whatever else he was, Brent was no coward." Cramp took another pull on his Scotch. "I'll let you know when we're going to get together to draw up a plan for the leadership. The way I figure it, we'll have three or four to choose from."

~

When Tom got back to his own office, his secretary told him someone had been trying to reach him.

"Who was it?"

"Lucile," said the secretary.

Tom's mind was blank, and he stared vacantly at the woman. Then he realized the reference to *The Rehearsal* and knew that Heidi was trying to reach him.

He withdrew into his office and made the call. "Hi, sweetheart, what's up?"

"They've taken Mom to hospital."

"Oh, no!"

"Her heart's been shaky for years. So with the strain and all, it's not surprising, I guess. But the doctor says it could have been a lot worse."

"I am so sorry to hear this, darling. Where are you now?"

"At the Infirmary. On the sixth floor."

"I'll come over right now and pick you up."

"Make it in half an hour. I'm going to look in on Mom again before I go."

Against all the hospital rules, Heidi had been taking the call from Tom in the corridor outside her mother's room. Just as she was taking her phone down from her ear, Anthony came out of the room.

"That was Aldridge, wasn't it?"

"Butt out, Anthony," Heidi said curtly.

"You've got to stop seeing him."

"Mind your own business."

"Listen to me, Heidi," Anthony said sternly. "Mom may be stable now, but she's still on the critical list. If she found out what was going on between you and Aldridge, it could kill her!"

Heidi, in tears, watched Anthony stalk away towards the elevators. When she had dried her eyes she went in to see her mother.

Florence was propped up in bed and was attached to a variety of tubes and instruments. She looked white and very frail.

"Mom, I'm going to head out now. I'll be back later."

"Are you going back to the house?" Florence's voice was faint and raspy.

"No, I'm going to see a friend."

"Not Tom Aldridge, I hope."

Heidi looked away, studying the dials and monitors.

"Heidi."

"Yes, Mom?"

"Are you going to see Tom Aldridge?"

"Why, what poison has Anthony been spreading now?"

"Please answer my question."

'Yes," said Heidi softly.

"I can't imagine what you find to do together. I mean, what do you have in common now the play is over?" Florence was hoarse. "I always thought you were a sensible girl. You should be very careful with a man like that. How old is he? Forty, fifty?"

"Forty-five, I think," Heidi answered in a whisper.

"Well, there you are, then. I don't want you getting involved."

"I won't. We're just friends."

"In my experience, a man and woman who see each other often don't stay 'just friends' for very long."

The tears started to stream down Heidi's cheeks.

"Promise me you won't get involved with Tom Aldridge." Florence's voice had become much weaker. "Promise me, Heidi. Promise!"

Heidi was silent.

"Promise!"

Heidi looked around the room, then back at her mother's drawn face. "I promise," she said, barely audibly.

When she came out of the room an orderly came up to her.

"Hey, honey. Are you Heidi?"

"Yes, that's me."

"A man's been waiting for you. Your father, is it?"

Heidi was taken aback with surprise and disgust as she tried to comprehend what the orderly was saying.

"My father's dead," she said.

"Sorry, honey. I didn't know. Oh, this is him now."

Turning round, Heidi saw Tom coming towards her. She was overwhelmed with discomfort and foreboding. Meekly, she followed him out to his car and sat quietly in the passenger seat.

"I've got your favourite pasta for supper," said Tom when they were on the road.

"I don't want to eat, Tom. I'm too tired."

"Okay, sweetheart. We'll just go home and have a drink."

"Didn't you hear me, Tom? I'm tired, please take me home. To the house,"

"What's wrong, darling?"

"It's all too much. I can't handle it. I need to be by myself for a while. Pull over, Tom."

"I can understand that," Tom said tenderly, easing the car to the curb. "I'll give you some space. But let me know when all this horrible stuff is over, and our time will come again."

"Maybe our time is past," said Heidi quietly.

Before he could respond, she got out of the car and walked away.

35

Tom was again plunged into despair, a condition worsened by Heidi's not returning any of his phone calls. He supposed that something as traumatic as her father's death would naturally, and seriously, upset her equilibrium, but he sensed that something else, new and decisive, had occurred to push her into breaking with him. Though he racked his brains, he could not imagine what that was.

In his misery, he called Blaine in New York, and pursuant to the latter's instructions related, word for word, his last conversation with Heidi.

"I think you're right," said Blaine. "Something happened between your phone conversation and your arrival at the hospital. We could speculate all day and still not know what it was. Did you do or say anything which might have been offensive to her?"

"No. Of course not."

"Then it will remain a mystery. It need not have been anything major, or even logical. After all, you can't really expect a twenty-five-year-old whose father has drowned and whose mother is in hospital to be entirely rational."

"No, I guess not."

"But one thing is clear, Tom. Assuming this could be resolved—which is by no means a given—there is nothing you can do. Nothing."

"But—"

"Anything you do now to pursue her will only make matters much worse. You must leave her completely alone. Time will tell whether this is a temporary break or a permanent severance. If you don't hear from her within the next two months, you must assume that it is over for good."

"It'll be damnably difficult, but I know you're right."

"Get yourself a new project and throw yourself into it," Blaine urged. "Keep your mind and body fully occupied. Is there anything like that on the horizon?"

"Actually, there is. The party will be having a leadership contest fairly soon. That could be time-consuming."

"Well, there's your answer."

~

Later that day, Ernest Maddingly summoned his cabinet. He knew that, whatever the ultimate outcome of a leadership contest, at least for the present he was a caretaker premier, so he had kept Granger's cabinet members, while making some adjustments in their portfolios.

When Granger became premier, he made a number of significant changes to the way things had traditionally been done and some of these affected the way the Whip had been viewed. Instead of having one whip who got his or her position as consolation prize for not making the cabinet, he appointed a Chief Whip and four regional whips, one each for Western Nova Scotia, South Shore and the Annapolis Valley; Halifax County; Northern and Eastern; and Cape Breton. These had the task of not only making sure all MLAs were in their seats when they were needed to speak or vote, but to know every intimate detail of the trials and problems of the Members in their areas.

The regional whips made this information available to the Chief

Whip, who kept meticulous records, and was able to report to the Premier back bench gossip, who was awkward, who was wayward, and who was loyal and well behaved. This made the Chief Whip an important person in the government and a cabinet minister without portfolio.

Another change Granger had made when he became premier was to move the cabinet to a much bigger room and to have a large, circular table installed. For its first few meetings, his cabinet had sat at the long narrow table in a long narrow room which had been used for years. Not only did this create congestion, but it meant it was not always possible for the premier to see who wished to speak on a given subject. Under his new arrangement he could, as he once told Arthur Cramp, "see the whites of their eyes."

Inevitably, thereafter the cabinet became known as the Knights of the Round Table.

In sequence, to Maddingly's right sat Angela Staples, the Minister of Justice and Attorney General; Minister of Economic Development Mark Gardiner; Wendell Proctor, Minister of Labour; Angus MacKinnon, Minister of Transport and Public Works; Minister of Agriculture and Fisheries Chretien Cormier; Stephanie Gilmour, Minister of Community Services, Tom Aldridge, Chief Whip; Harland MacIvor, Minister of Tourism and Culture; Fiona MacPherson, Minister of Municipal Affairs and Housing; Minister of the Environment Leona Beals; Education Minister Albany Boudreau; Minister of Health Kesegoo'e Sillyboy, and Minister of Finance Chester Mac-Cormack.

That meant that Tom's seat was directly opposite the premier on the far side of the circle, from where he could easily signal the premier if a subject was raised which was potentially dangerous, sensitive or embarrassing.

Maddingly opened the meeting and plunged straight into business before Stephanie interrupted, suggesting that it would be proper to commence with three minutes' silence to honour their previous chief.

"Of course, of course," Maddingly muttered. He stood up and bowed his head.

Everybody followed suit. Tom squinted to see how many were actually bowed in prayer and how many were killing time by looking around the room.

The Ministers who appeared to be most sincere were Cormier, Boudreau, MacIvor and Stephanie herself. Wendell looked uncomfortable, keeping his hands on the table. Leona Beals was gently swaying from side to side. Most of the others were staring at the ceiling.

Maddingly, obviously overdoing it for effect, held his head so others might see his lips moving in soundless prayer.

The long three minutes completed and everybody back in their seats, the new premier informed the cabinet that the party officers had decided to hold a leadership contest in forty days. He said that they had decided on an old fashioned convention, and had rejected the modern fad for a preferential ballot system. There would be a run-off, with the candidate with the fewest votes dropping off the ballot in each round, until the last vote would be between the two front runners.

"Hooray," Wendell said loudly. "I hate that preferential balloting. It meant the winner was someone nobody wants, but was the least hated."

An appreciative laugh ran around the table. It seemed Wendell's opinion was shared by most.

"And it's the best way for a nonentity to come through the pack," said Chester MacCormack.

"I hope you're not referring to me," Maddingly said indignantly.

There was an embarrassed shuffling, as the ministers looked away, or started rummaging in their briefcases. Wendell gave Tom a wide-eyed look of disbelief. Someone, Tom thought it was Angus MacKinnon, was laughing quietly but uncontrollably.

"Good heavens, no, premier!" MacCormack said. "Whatever would make you think such a thing?"

"Order! Quiet!" Maddingly commanded. "Let's get on. Forty days is enough for the constituencies to choose their delegates and register them with the party office. I'm told that the Nova Centre has already been booked and that, provisionally, the party has also booked 400 rooms in local hotels. Are there any questions?"

"Yes, premier." It was Mark Gardiner. "What if members of the cabinet wish to become candidates? Would they have to resign?"

"Oh God!" Maddingly exclaimed. "I hadn't thought of that. If the contest were further off, I might say 'yes'. But, frankly, I think it would cause chaos under the present circumstances. I hope we can count on those ministers who do enter the race to act with discretion and not exploit their ministerial positions. I shall inform the Departmental Deputy Ministers to keep an eye out for any shenanigans of that kind."

"Shall you be entering the race yourself, premier?" asked Angus MacKinnon in a sing-song voice.

"I have many heavy responsibilities to attend to, without having time to think about that," Maddingly said sternly.

"But if you were urged by your colleagues,"—MacKinnon looked around the table—"would you succumb to pressure and make yourself available?"

"Well, under those conditions, one might have to accept the burden," Maddingly said, completely missing MacKinnon's note of sarcasm.

A few ministers applauded. Most did not. The meeting descended into disorder as they all started talking at once.

Wendell sent a note to Tom which was passed around the table. Rudely, MacKinnon opened and read it. He raised his eyebrows and scribbled on the note, then passed it on.

It read: "Council of War. Summoned by Uncle Arthur. Speaker's Office. An hour."

Underneath was scrawled: "Good. I'll be there!"

When they filed into the Speakers office, Cramp was clearly surprised to see MacKinnon among them. His eyes narrowed and his lips tightened. Tom, Wendell, Stephanie, Sam McNeil, Chester Mac-Cormack, Speaker Bill Clark, a Senator, Gabriel Carvery, Zandili, and the party secretary, Madeline Snow were crammed into chairs and on window ledges.

"Hello, Angus. I didn't expect to see you here," Cramp said quietly.

"Well, you know, Arthur, I have the party's best interests at heart. So when I discovered that the wheelers and dealers were meeting, I wanted to be on it."

"Fair enough. Take a seat and grab yourself a Scotch, anyone who can reach it."

There was a chaotic scramble of people moving, passing the whisky bottle and glasses and, in some cases, squatting on the floor.

"I won't keep you long, and I'll get straight to the point. The people in this room have the combined influence to sway a convention and elect the next leader. If, and I repeat if, we are united on the candidate and get behind him or her a hundred percent."

There was a muttering of general agreement.

Cramp took a swig of Scotch, then continued. "But if we are divided, any asshole could win it. That means we all have to agree to support whoever is the majority choice of the group. No breaking away and going for it on your own. Understood?"

Everyone indicated their agreement except MacKinnon.

"I am not sure I'd be prepared to give that assurance this early in the game, Arthur."

"Then you've got to leave the group. We can't be doing anything with any fifth columnists." Cramp was firm. "And once you leave, there may not be any way you can come back."

"Understood."

"And, Angus...that means if you run and our choice should be knocked out, there's no guarantee we would shift our support to you."

"Ah," said MacKinnon. "let me think about it. I'll get back to you, Arthur."

"Well, don't leave it too long. The door might not stay open."

"Okay."

"Alright, children. Get busy. Go rustle the bushes and report back. I may call another meeting after the funeral. Remember, Brent is being buried tomorrow. I expect to see every one of you in attendance."

~

That evening was the first time since her father's death that Heidi had been back to her apartment. She felt she should stay around the family home until her mother was discharged from hospital, but she needed to pick up some underwear and toiletries.

She had hoped nobody would be home when she dropped by, but when she inserted her key and pushed open the door, she saw both Leslie and Francine drinking wine at the kitchen table. They rushed to her, hugging, kissing and commiserating.

"You poor thing," said Francine. "You must have gone through absolute hell."

"But you're back with your friends now," Leslie added. "Sit down and have a glass of wine with us."

"Alright, but I can't stay long. I have to see Mom at the hospital later."

"How is she, Heidi?"

"'In critical but stable condition' is what the doctors told me. I'm not exactly sure what that means, but she's conscious and able to talk, though she seems very weak."

"It's been so much to put on your shoulders, honey," Leslie said.

"The twins are a mess, of course, but Anthony is stepping up and taking care of a lot of the details. It's Dad's funeral tomorrow."

"We know. We'll be there, if we can get in."

Heidi took the glass of wine from Francine and sat down at the table. She took a sip and looked around. Everything was perfectly familiar but also strange. She no longer felt she belonged there.

"Oh, Heidi," said Leslie, "that Tom has been calling here day and night. I told him you weren't here but he keeps trying. What's going on there?"

"I don't want to talk about it," said Heidi, tetchily.

"Are you and he not copacetic any longer?"

"What happened, Heid?"

Heidi shook her head crossly, and put her wine down with a bang. "What part of 'I don't want to talk about it' did you not understand?" she demanded angrily.

She jumped up, went to her room, and collected the necessary items. Leslie and Francine sat looking at each other, afraid to say another word.

Heidi came back into the kitchen and, seizing her jacket, stormed out of the apartment. As she clattered down the stairs and into the street, tears streamed down her cheeks.

36

Never had there been a funeral like it in the province. Historians said it was likely the biggest funeral held in Halifax since that of Sir John Thompson in 1895.

Sir John, a native of Halifax and a surprisingly-early supporter of women's rights, had been premier for only two months before being defeated at the polls by the Liberals' Thomas Pipes. When he became Prime Minister, his luck was almost as bad, his serving in that office for barely two years before dying of a heart attack while visiting Queen Victoria at Windsor Castle. Feeling unwell, apparently, he had drunk a glass of brandy, saying "I'm all right, now, than'you." Those were his last words as he unceremoniously crashed to the floor.

When his body was brought back to Nova Scotia on *HMS Blenheim*, thousands lined the streets and an immensely elaborate funeral service was held.

Since no Nova Scotian had lived beyond the age of a hundred and thirty, exact comparisons between the Thompson and Granger funerals were not possible. But it was incontestable that, today, the cathedral was so full it would literally have been impossible to shoehorn another person through the huge wooden doors. In fact, the doors could not even be closed because those out on the steps crowded the entrance. Close to five hundred people thronged the sidewalk and others stood, straining to hear, on the other side of the street.

Inside, every seat was taken, and mourners were standing shoulder to shoulder at the back of the nave. Despite the lofty ceiling, the atmosphere had already started to become hot, stuffy and oppressive.

In the aisle, next to the front row of pews, was Florence Granger in a wheelchair. They had allowed her out of hospital for the occasion, but had insisted she return immediately after the service. A male nurse sat just behind and to her left in case the need arose for medical attention.

In the front row, on the left of the aisle, sat Anthony, Heidi, Poppy, Petra, and several aunts and uncles. The front row on the other side of the aisle was occupied by the new premier, Maddingly; the Speaker, Bill Clark; Cramp; both opposition party leaders; Sam McNeil; and Madeline Snow.

In the next few rows were various members of the cabinet and the legislature, including Wendall, Stephanie, Zandili, Angela Staples, Mark Gardiner, Angus MacKinnon, Chretien Cormier, Harland MacIvor, Leona Beals, Albany Boudreau, Fiona MacPherson, and Senator Carvery. Kessegoo'e Sillyboy and Chester MacCormack had been late arriving and had to be satisfied with seats behind a pillar at the rear.

Elsewhere, dotted about the congregation, were Cynthia, Andrew, Chedva, Sarah, Mathew and Grace. Appearances suggested that Leslie and Francine had been unable to obtain admittance.

Tom deliberately stayed standing at the back, just inside the doors. He was feeling desolate, a condition intensified by the sadness of the occasion. It filled him with emotion that he would be in the same place as Heidi, but far away from her.

The powerful music of Bach's *Toccata and Fugue in D Minor*, chosen by Heidi, soared among the stone columns and up into the intricately vaulted roof, the bass notes faintly rattling the panes in the neo-Gothic stained glass windows through which long shafts of light were streaming down, as though they were messages from Heaven.

The archbishop gave a homily of a general but uplifting nature, then Arthur Cramp was called on to deliver the eulogy. He stood, hunched, and tired, looking even older than his eighty-two years.

With tears in his eyes, in a raspy, but audible voice Cramp spoke of the Brenton Granger he had known as a soldier, a surgeon, a family man, and as a premier. "He was the best. That's all there is to it," Cramp said firmly. "He was my best friend. The best leader. The best of men. There will never be another like him."

Then, in a delivery which was strong and dignified, Anthony rose to say that his father had been an inspiration to him through-out his life, always ready to listen, always ready to give advice, and that he would always be very greatly missed by all who knew him.

In what many thought was a meretricious display, Poppy and Petra, the twins, read out what others thought was a tasteless and inapposite poem:

> *I'm not gone.*
> *So don't stop being you, carry on.*
> *If you meet someone new,*
> *I'll still hold your hand.*
> *I'm always with you, by your side.*
> *I still breathe in your perfume*
> *and run my fingers through your hair.*
> *Soon we'll be together,*
> *But until then,*
> *Take care.*

The problem was compounded by their not being able to syn-chronize their speech, so they tumbled over one another's words, ending in a semi-giggling state of embarrassment.

The congregation was invited to sing *When I Survey the Wondrous Cross*, which had been one of Brenton's favourites, and a little later *Abide With Me*, a hymn he had often told his children was being played on the *Titanic* when she went down in 1912.

At that point, Heidi was called on to read a lesson. She chose I Corinthians 1. Tom strained to see her, edging between a tall and a fat woman. She looked pale, but so very beautiful she almost took his breath away.

Her voice was clear as a bell and reached every corner of the cathedral.

Love never fails. But where there are prophecies, they will cease; where there are tongues, they will be stilled; where there is knowledge, it will pass away. For we know in part and we prophesy in part, but when completeness comes, what is in part disappears.

When I was a child, I talked like a child, I thought like a child, I reasoned like a child. When I became a man, I put the ways of childhood behind me.

For now we see only a reflection as in a mirror; then we shall see face to face. Now I know in part; then I shall know fully, even as I am fully known.

And now these three remain: faith, hope and love. But the greatest of these is love.

On hearing this last line, Tom could not help himself, and started sobbing into his handkerchief. Those around him who recognized him assumed he had been particularly devoted to his former chief.

The Archbishop rose again, thanked all for coming to pay tribute to a great Nova Scotian, gave the Benediction and discharged the congregation.

"May the Lord bless you and keep you; the Lord make his face shine upon you and be gracious unto you; the Lord turn his face toward you and give you peace."

Everyone stood while first the coffin, and then the mourners in the reverse order of their seating, filed quietly out. Following the pall bearers came Anthony pushing Florence's wheel chair, then the rest of the family.

As the procession passed him, Tom looked longingly at Heidi, who gave him the slightest glance out the corner of her eye. Once the family had exited, he slipped away and pushed through the doors to the outside. He watched the family getting into their limousines, Florence with some difficulty.

After Heidi helped her mother, and turned to go to the other side of the car, she noticed Tom standing on the steps. Without raising her arm, she made the barest gesture with her black-gloved hand, and then took her seat. The hearse pulled away and the other vehicles followed.

Nobody noticed that the premier's devoted chauffeur, Parsons, had not been in attendance at the funeral of his long-time friend and master.

37

The morning following Brenton Granger's funeral, Ernest Maddingly was having breakfast of weak tea, cream of wheat and brown toast with honey. As he was contemplating having a second piece of toast, his phone rang. He was annoyed to be bothered at home, and his first instinct was to ignore the call.

"You should take it, Ernie," said his wife, Gladys. "It might be important. After all, you are premier now."

"Yes, of course, you're right."

He picked up the phone and pressed the button. "Premier Maddingly speaking."

"Ernie, this is Arthur."

"Oh, hello, Arthur. What can I do for you?"

"I was wondering if a group of us could come to see you tomorrow."

"A group? What is this all about?"

"We're now about thirty, including cabinet members, MLAs and party bigwigs."

"A deputation?"

"You could call it that. We want to discuss the leadership."

"Ah!" Maddingly was suddenly interested and alert. "Well, yes, of course. Good idea. My office is large enough to accommodate that many, but I'll need Mrs. Wilson to get more chairs."

"You do that. Get her to lay on some coffee and sandwiches, too. We'll be there around noon," Cramp said perfunctorily, and hung

193

up.

"Well!" Maddingly said to his wife. "I must say, I don't much like the way Arthur Cramp treats me. I think I deserve a little more respect."

"You certainly do," said Gladys. "That Cramp is a crusty old so-and-so. You put him in his place next time you see him."

"I'll probably see him later today. He's always hanging around Province House."

Maddingly drained his teacup and rose from the table. He started to leave when a thought struck him. "Gladys, shouldn't I have a car and chauffeur now?"

"Yes, of course you should. Granger had a limousine driven by that horrible little Parsons."

"Would you call Mrs. Wilson and have her send the car out? I think I might have another cup of tea while I'm waiting."

Maddingly sat down again, refilled his cup and stretched out in the chair. Of course, he thought, he should have every benefit and perquisite due to the Premier of Nova Scotia, and he would make sure he received them.

Gladys came back into the room, a puzzled look on her face. "Mrs. Wilson says there is no sign of Parsons. He did not report for work this morning, so she called his lodgings."

"So where is he?"

"She said he had checked out of the boarding house, and nobody knows where he went."

"What a nuisance. Who's the back-up driver?"

"Mrs. Wilson says there isn't one. Apparently, you have to appoint your own chauffeur. She said it used to be handled by Transport and Public Works, but Granger changed that."

"Damn him! The family car is in the shop. You'd better call me a taxi, Gladys."

"Alright, Ernie. And you make sure the government reimburses you for the fare."

~

As Maddingly's taxi was pulling into the Province House yard, Arthur Cramp and Tom Aldridge were on the steps, chatting.

"We've got to move this thing along," Cramp said. "So you'll be there?"

"What time?"

"Come to Maddingly's office about noon tomorrow."

"I'll be there. See you then."

At that moment, Maddingly got out of the taxi and, coming up to them, put his arms around their shoulders.

"My loyal friends," he said cheerily, "how am I doing? Pretty good so far, wouldn't you say, boys?"

"You've only been there for five minutes, Ernie," Cramp growled, "but so far you've managed to stay out of trouble."

"I'll take that as a compliment, coming from you, Arthur. How about you, Tom?"

"No serious problems, premier."

"I think I've surprised a good many people. I rather think the citizens of the province, and our party members, will be inclined to approve."

Condescendingly, he patted both of them on the back. He then swept away, through Province House, to his office on the other side of the building, pausing only to glare at the limousine which was parked nearby.

"Did you listen to that asshole? You know what that was all about, don't you? That sonofabitch intends to run for the leadership. He wants to stay as premier."

"You think so? He can't win. Can he?"

"Over my fucking dead body," said Cramp with great feeling. "We may as well get Harpo Marx. Tom, we will nip this lunacy in the bud tomorrow. I'll be fucked if that senile, aristocratic buffoon is going to be the leader of my party! Will you make sure your crowd is there?"

"Sure. I'll see Stephanie tonight, and call the others."

"Good."

"Arthur..."

"What?"

"Do you want me to call Angus MacKinnon?"

"No, leave him to me."

~

Stephanie Gilmour was a beautiful, classy woman of thirty-seven. She was highly intelligent, had a well-developed sense of humour, and excellent taste in clothes, jewellery, wine and food. She was also very rich, having inherited several millions from her father, the head of the province's largest law firm. He had also been a political person, though not elected, was a Senator, and had represented both provincial and federal governments in overseas business deals.

It might be unkind to suggest that Stephanie could afford her liberal views more easily than someone not blessed with wealth and social position. However, a glance at her home, in the south end of the city, confirmed the impression that her political opinions had been formed in comfort rather than in adversity.

Her house, elevated from the street, was a large, multi-level structure built before World War Two, when Frank Lloyd Wright was still designing individual homes for those who could afford his fees. While impressive, the house seemed somewhat anachronistic and more dated than surrounding homes which were actually older, but it was a local landmark and still had a certain flair and dignity.

There was a large forecourt bisected by a driveway which al-most doubled back on itself. This gave the impression of ascending a small mountain. Tom cruised up this steeply inclined, rock-lined feature and parked in front.

Stephanie was waiting at the door. She led him inside to a large room with floor-to-ceiling windows, thick Axminster carpets, and low, soft divans. Stephanie said she had Champagne if he would like it, but Tom, spoiled by many visits to Chedva, said he would prefer a Scotch. She poured him a glass of eighteen-year-old Glen-goyne Highland malt which, contrary to all the strictures of the purists, he took with a little soda.

Stephanie, always good looking, tonight was exceptionally beau-tiful. She was wearing a simple, white silk dress which revealed al-most as much as it hid, and softly rustled as she moved. Her small items of plain gold jewellery were clearly as expensive as they were tasteful.

Apart from when he had been with Blaine, Tom could not re-member a meal as good as the one Stephanie served him that night. There was steamed Faroe Island salmon to start, napped with a *beurre blanc*, followed by a roasted guinea fowl with wild mushrooms. She knew Tom was not a huge fan of dessert, so she had a cheese board of Brillat Savarin, Valency, Hercule de Charle-voix, Riopelle and Pieds de vent, which she obtained from Ratin-aud, a French delicatessen on Gottingen Street which she regularly frequented.

Stephanie served a 2016 Savennieres, Clos du Papillon with the salmon, a 2009 Clos des Mouches with the guinea fowl and a 2012 Bâtard-Montrachet with the cheese. Tom was surprised to be served a white wine with cheese, but he found the combination to be perfect, far better than red wine would have provided.

It was not until they were back on the divan that Tom began to realize that the whole evening had been an attempt at seduction, and when Stephanie leaned over and kissed him, he pulled away and started to weep.

"Please don't be insulted, Steph. It's just that I'm hurting so much over losing Heidi."

"Heidi?" Stephanie was alert. "You don't mean the Granger girl?"

Tom nodded.

"Oh, you poor man. I can see the attraction. She's very beautiful, but very, very young."

Tom nodded again.

"You know I'm not a disinterested party, Tom. But you must remember that at that age they fall out of love as fast and as easily as they fall in love. If I were you I would try to forget her."

38

Tom was unable to get much sleep, so he rose early the next morning and walked to work. He found himself being drawn off-route in the direction of St. Michael's and, before he knew it, he was standing in front of the church and its hall. The sign board still bore a tattered notice for *The Rehearsal*.

This place and its associations overwhelmed him and visions of Heidi, in costume as Lucille, flashed across his mind.

"Tom?"

He snapped out of his reverie and looked to see Father Geoffrey in the church doorway. "Father Geoffrey. Good morning."

"What are you doing in this neck of the woods? Revisiting the site of your great triumph?"

"My great tragedy, more like."

"Tragedy?"

"It's a long story, Father, but my girlfriend has broken up with me."

"Ah. Was it what I suspected?"

"How do you mean?"

"I could see you falling for that lovely, young girl. So you did manage to get together?"

"For a while, yes."

"And now, the pangs of lost love?"

"Something like that."

"But you are still alive," said Father Geoffrey sententiously, "and

God will give you other chances of happiness."

"She was the love of my life. I'll never forget her."

"Possibly not. But mooning about in a self-pitying way is very unbecoming, Tom. It will do you no good, and will drive your friends away from you. If you'll take my advice, you will keep your lamentations to yourself, and move on."

~

Around ten o'clock that morning, Florence Granger was discharged from hospital with strict instructions that she assiduously take her medications, not exert herself in any way, get lots of rest, and eat a simple diet. The attending physician told Anthony and Heidi, who were there to take her home, that Florence was much improved; but from her appearance, Heidi thought she looked weaker and older.

The doctor said that her husband's funeral had not had the exacerbating effect they feared, told them what signs to look for if their mother's condition deteriorated and, in that event, what action they should take.

"Heidi, have you gone back to work yet?" her mother asked when they were in the car.

"No, Mom. I thought I would stay off a bit longer to look after you."

"That will not be necessary," Florence said firmly. "You go back tomorrow. I'll be fine."

"If you're sure."

"I am sure."

When they arrived at the house, Anthony got out first in order to retrieve the collapsed wheelchair from the trunk.

When he was at the rear of the vehicle, Florence whispered to Heidi. "Have you kept your promise?"

"Promise?" asked Heidi, knowing full well to what her mother was referring.

"Your promise not to get involved with Tom Aldridge."

"Yes."

"Not even seen him?"

"No."

"Good. Let's keep it that way."

~

Tom spent the morning phoning colleagues, urging the closer ones to attend the noon meeting, and sounding out the others as to their current thinking about the leadership. There was nothing he could put his finger on, but, for reasons he couldn't fathom, almost all of them seemed much friendlier than usual. At eleven forty-five, Wendell arrived and they walked together to the premier's office.

"This should be fun," said Wendell.

"It could get dirty. Uncle Arthur is out for blood."

"It depends how he handles it. He can be a vicious grizzly bear, but he can also be an old smoothie when he wants to be."

"Yes, that's true," Tom said, "and today would be the day for the stiletto rather than the axe."

The premier's office was packed to the rafters. While extra chairs had been brought in, many people were standing and some, like Zandili, were sitting on the floor.

The premier's secretary, Mrs. Wilson, squeezed between the bodies, passing plates of sandwiches. Then she wheeled in a trolley containing a coffee urn and cups, but finding nowhere to put it, left it in the open doorway.

Maddingly was benign and patronizing, smiling and shaking every hand. It was apparent that, whether as a result of wishful thinking or by Cramp's deliberate misrepresentation, he had convinced himself that the gathering had been called to endorse his own candidacy for leader.

He appeared to be presiding over the meeting, but it soon became clear that it was not he, but Cramp, who was really in charge.

"Order, please!" said Maddingly after taking his seat behind the shiny rosewood desk. "Thank you all for coming. It was good of you to come at such short notice. That is a gesture which is not unappreciated. The purpose of this gathering is to discuss the future. The future of the party and of the province. These are matters of no small importance to all of us."

He cleared his throat and took a sip of water.

"Since it was largely at the instigation of our good friend, Arthur Cramp, that we are assembled, I shall ask him to address us. Arthur, if you'd be so kind...."

"Thank you Ernie. Just to recap for those who are new to the group. None of us knows what a convention will do, but—let's face it—the people in this room are the movers and shakers in the party. We can't guarantee someone's election, but we sure as hell might be able stop someone we don't want."

There were murmurs of agreement around the room. Maddingly sat unruffled, a paternal smile permanently fixed to his face.

"These are the rules. Anybody who doesn't like them or won't abide by them should leave. There will be no hard feelings, but once you go, you're gone. Let me be clear: When the group has a nominee, we all get behind that person until the bitter end."

Not a person moved towards the door, and several nodded vigorously in agreement. A slight frown appeared on Maddingly's face and his smile weakened.

"In that connection, I spoke to Angus MacKinnon just before the meeting. He won't be joining us because he says he doesn't want to limit his options. The translation of that is that he will be a candidate!"

A hearty laugh ran through the company. Zandili's cackle could clearly be heard above the others.

"What about you, Art?" Madeline Snow asked very deliberately. She had been primed to ask this very question.

"Let's get real. I'm far too old. This is a job for a much younger man. Much younger."

A glimmer of discomfort crossed Maddingly's face.

"Maybe it's time for a black premier," said Senator Carvery.

"Maybe," said Cramp.

"Or a woman," offered Zandili from the floor.

"Also a possibility."

"Excuse me," said Maddingly rather weakly, "but what about the incumbent?"

"Wouldn't be fair to you Ernie," said Madeline Snow.

Her comment received a loud murmur of assent.

"We couldn't ask you to make that kind of sacrifice at your time of life, Ernie. You've served a good many years and you deserve a rest."

Several in the room said, "Hear, hear!"

"In fact," Madeline continued, "I'm going to call on the meeting for a round of applause for Ernest Maddingly who, against his own interests, stepped into the breach to do his duty to his party and the province."

The applause was as thunderous as it was obviously hypocritical, but Maddlingly got the message loud and clear, and sank back in his chair a beaten man.

"Now then," said Cramp, retaking control, "I spent yesterday, canvassing not only the members of this group, but also other activists around the province and I asked them to rate possible contenders. I gave them eight names—not necessarily the best eight people—but the eight most likely to have enough support to go forward to the convention."

This announcement clearly met with the approval of the group.

"Read us the list, Arthur," said Madeline Snow.

"The names won't surprise you," said Cramp, "but the order of preference might."

Virtually the whole room was chanting, "Read the list! Read the list!"

"Okay, okay. At the top of the list, the favourite of those contacted is..."

Cramp paused for dramatic effect. The room went wild, shouting "Name! Name!"

"Alright. Number one on the list is Tom Aldridge."

A loud cheer went up from well over half the room.

When he heard it, Tom was thunderstruck and thought Uncle Arthur was making a sick joke. He knew that, in his present state of mind, he was not equal to the task ahead.

"Let me read the whole list before I ask for responses from the candidates. Okay, here it is: Number One, Tom Aldridge. Number Two Chester MacCormack. Number Three, Wendell Proctor. Number Four, Stephanie Gilmour. Number Five, Bill Clark. Number six, Kesegoo'e Sillyboy, Number Seven, Leona Beals, and Number Eight, Fiona MacPherson."

The room was abuzz with excitement. Some names were surprises, others not. The order of preference was unexpected but, on reflection, understandable.

"I will now ask, in order, those on the list if they will stand. Please be clear, once a person has agreed to stand, the others are in honour bound not to run themselves and to get behind the winner."

Arthur Cramp moved from the edge of the desk and faced Tom.

"Tom, will you accept?"

"No. I won't. I can't. I'm not ready. I don't know if I'd ever be ready for something like this."

"Alright. Fair enough. Chester, will you accept."

"I appreciate the support of so many friends, but as you said yourself, Art, this is a job for a younger person. I'll be fifty-nine next birthday."

"Okay, Wendell. How about you? Will you accept?"

"Yes sir," said Wendell happily, "I most surely will."

The room erupted with loud applause and cheering. Zandili was singing "We Shall Overcome."

"Alright everybody." Cramp had to shout to make himself heard. "This is our candidate. This, and no other, unless he should be knocked off the ballot at some stage of the convention. You are all bound by our agreement today, and we expect you to give one hundred percent backing. Wendell, do you know who your campaign manager will be yet?"

"Yes sir. Tom, if he'll do it."

"Wendell is my best friend. I pledge to give him everything I have," said Tom to more cheers.

"Good. Then we are adjourned!"

Arthur Cramp left the premier's office a very happy man. A good day's work had been accomplished, and it had all gone according to plan.

39

There was no time to lose. Tom had barely five weeks to organize Wendell's campaign and put his man over the top.

The first thing he did—on Arthur Cramp's suggestion—was to leak to the media the names of all those who had attended the meeting in Maddingly's office, and to make sure that it became public knowledge that they had all agreed to back Wendell's candidacy to the bitter end. That way, he thought, it would be impossible for any of them to renege on the deal without appearing to be thoroughly dishonourable.

Tom secured more than adequate campaign headquarters in an empty store on Quinpool Road which was adjacent to a parking area, then ordered ten telephone lines to be installed on a priority basis. The costs were high, but they could afford them since donations were already pouring in.

The first public event he organized was a press conference at which Wendell formally announced his candidacy. On either side of Wendell stood Chester MacCormack, the Minister of Finance, and Stephanie.

Next to Chester was Environment Minister Leona Beals, then the Speaker, Bill Clark. Next to Stephanie stood Kesegoo'e Sillyboy and then Fiona MacPherson, Minister of Municipal Affairs. Prominently situated behind Wendell were Senator Carvery and Madeline Snow.

The arrangement was, in Cramp's cynical words, a "masterly

balance of colour," since it alternated between Caucasians and members of visible minorities.

Tom had wanted to include Ernest Maddingly in the press conference, but felt that to ask him would be adding insult to injury. Besides, if he had asked and Maddingly refused, and it got out to the press, it would be a bad start to Wendell's campaign. It was better to leave Ernie alone. He had only five more weeks of being the premier: Let him enjoy it while he could.

Each of the province's fifty-two constituencies was entitled to send twenty delegates to the convention. In addition, the forty-one government MLAs, the provincial party's officers and executive, and MPs and Senators each had the right to be *ex officio* delegates. Assuming they all showed up, Tom calculated that eleven hundred and thirteen people were eligible to vote.

He figured that Wendell was strongest in Halifax County, containing some eighteen constituencies, where he was best known, and in Pictou and Colchester counties, containing a further eight constituencies, where he had many family connections. Apart from Sydney itself, he was weakest in Cape Breton and the south-western end of the province.

Assuming that the attendees at the meeting which had selected him could influence a fair share of delegates in their areas, Tom thought he could find at least three hundred and fifty votes for Wendell on the first ballot, with strong potential for growth. Whether the opportunity for that growth would present itself would depend on how many others entered the race and, of course, who they would be.

He did not have long to wait. Mark Gardiner was next to join the race. Gardiner was young, good looking, but generally considered to be brash and self-centred. Also, as he was Minister of Economic Development, his reputation had suffered somewhat in recent weeks due to his being, unfairly, blamed for a number of factory closures. Tom guessed that Gardiner would attract, at most, a hundred and twenty votes, and would drop off after the first ballot unless a weaker candidate got into the race.

Then, to almost everyone's surprise, including Tom's, Albany Boudreau announced his candidacy. Boudreau was very popular in the party for his "aww, shucks" manner of speaking, which was liberally larded with corny jokes. Also, contrary to most expectations, he had proved to be a highly competent Minister of Education. Boudreau could expect to harvest virtually all of the delegates in the four or five constituencies in which Acadians were in a majority or had a strong presence. Cramp's comment was to the effect that Boudreau would get the Acadian vote out of "tribal loyalty."

Assessing his strength was not easy. On paper, Tom could find only about a hundred votes on the first ballot, but he knew that Boudreau was exceedingly well liked as a thoroughly good person who was also entertaining on the hustings. Therefore, he provisionally put Boudreau at one hundred and seventy-five on the first ballot.

So far, things looked promising for Wendell, but there was a looming prospect which could change everything: Angus MacKinnon.

MacKinnon was an able, handsome, and ruthless (some said, unscrupulous) politician who was in great demand as a speaker at party events, second only to Brenton Granger himself. He had used his patronage opportunities as Minister of Transport and Public Works to punctiliously woo rural voters of the northern and eastern sections of the province, paying assiduous attention to secondary and tertiary roads. Were he a candidate, he could be expected to tie up the six constituencies in his area, together with four or five Cape Breton ridings. Tom thought MacKinnon was also bound to attract delegates from each of the other candidates in the early stages, but he wondered if his campaign was too slick, or he appeared too confident, it could be his undoing.

Was the man really sufficiently trusted, and would delegates stay with him if push came to shove? In any event, Tom had to conclude that, on the first ballot, MacKinnon could garner as many as four hundred votes.

In the meantime, Tom assigned a list of party supporters, all likely to be delegates, to each of those who attended the meeting in Maddingly's office. It would be their job to call, or preferably to see, the people on their list and to report back.

While he was wrestling with these matters, Wendell poked his head round the door.

"Can I come in?"

"These are your headquarters. Of course you can come in, you dope."

"I have some good news."

"That, I can use. What is it?"

"Cynthia and I are engaged and will be married in the New Year."

"That's marvellous! But how is that going down with Her Majesty?"

"Grace is as good as gold with it."

"Really? How come? Did Mathew work some kind of miracle?"

"Indeed he did," Wendell was laughing. "Do you recall how Huey Long got black nurses into Louisiana hospitals?"

"Not sure I do."

"Before his time, nursing was an all-white profession. So, Old Huey went around saying how the black men in the hospitals might commit outrages against the delicate white nurses. In no time at all, the state was hiring all kinds of black nurses to look after the black men!"

"Huh! Maybe Huey wasn't as bad as he was painted," Tom said. "But what's that got to do with you and Cynthia?"

"Matt is a sly old dog when he wants to be. When he found out I was running for the party leadership, he buttered Grace up, allowing as how she would be an even more important person if I should win, especially if I became premier."

"Go on."

"You're not going to believe this, and for God's sake don't tell anyone else."

"Okay, I promise."

"Matthew convinced her that my chances of winning would be increased if I had a white partner, and especially a white wife!"

"You're kidding? The man's a genius."

"Now she's going around, acting like Cynthia and I being together was all her idea in the first place. Cynthia is even invited to Sunday dinner!"

"That's wonderful, Wendell. I am very happy for you."

"It's too bad it can't be a double wedding."

"Yeah," Tom said sadly. "That would have been nice."

"Anyway," said Wendell, getting up and heading for the door. "I got things to do, places to go, people to see."

"Indeed you do. You won't get any votes hanging around here."

~

That same day, Heidi decided to move back into the family home. It was not only because she was concerned about her mother, who continued to be very frail, but because she could no longer stand to be around Leslie. Relations between them had been strained for some time, mostly because of her affair with Tom, but events of the previous night had been decisive.

She went to bed about eleven o'clock and had been asleep for some time, when she felt a presence in her bed. In that confused state between sleep and wakefulness, she imagined it was Tom who was caressing her breasts, but then she awoke with a start to find Leslie all over her.

"What the hell!"

"I was just trying to comfort you," said Leslie.

"Well, don't!"

"Just relax, Heidi, you'll enjoy it!"

"Fuck off, Leslie. Just fuck off!"

Heidi said she would collect her stuff when Leslie was out the next day, and that she would never see her again, at least not voluntarily.

She knew that life at home with the twins would be a trial, but she thought that she and Anthony had a better understanding since their father's death.

Her mother was surprised by the news, but pleased. She could not remember the last time she had a decent conversation, and now looked forward to renewing that pleasant pastime with her eldest daughter.

40

The next day Tom and Arthur were in the Headquarters when they heard the news on the radio. Angus MacKinnon had thrown his hat into the ring. That was no surprise, but what was a surprise was that Justice Minister Angela Staples and Tourism Minister Harland MacIvor were supporting him.

This struck Tom and Arthur as strange, because Staples had always ploughed a lonely furrow, forming neither friendships nor alliances, while MacIvor had never made any bones about his contempt for Mackinnon.

In mid-morning, when the place was empty, they looked up from their lists and maps to see that Joan Howard was standing before them. As always, she glowed with good health and fabulous beauty, which rendered most men very uneasy, sometimes reducing them to blubbering fools.

If she looked as if she had just stepped off the cover of Vogue or out of a Hollywood movie, it was because she had. Joan, originally from Nova Scotia, had left when she was eighteen, had gone to California and had made a name for herself as one of the most successful models and film actresses of her generation.

She had been shooting a movie in the province some three years previously when she met Harold Nickerson, who had been hired by the production to use his Cape Island boat in the film. Contrary to all expectations, they had fallen madly in love and married, whereupon Joan moved back to the province.

An even more unlikely event occurred a year later, when the local MLA died and Joan was adopted as the party candidate. She ran in the by-election and was elected by a razor-thin margin. Described by Cramp as "our own glamour puss", she sat on the very back bench in the house, constantly drawing all eyes in her direction.

Because she was a show-business personality, and because she had been elected in an opposition stronghold, she was not taken seriously as a politician. It was assumed that her election was a "freak" and that she would be defeated when the next general election was held. Neither Tom nor Arthur had even thought of inviting her to the meeting which selected Wendell, and had not given the slightest thought to trying to obtain her support.

"Joan!" Cramp's mouth fell open. "To what do we owe this honour?"

"I'm here to help," she said, her words coming like silk on a misty morning.

"Really?" Tom was flabbergasted.

"Of course. Why shouldn't I?"

"You're most welcome," said Cramp. "Any particular reason you're here?"

"I believe in Wendell Proctor!" Joan made it sound like the closing lines of *Gone with the Wind*.

"It's wonderful to hear you say that. How do you think you could help?"

"How about twenty thousand dollars, for a start?" Her words were like honey on a summer's day. She took her cheque book out of her Hermes purse.

"Holy cow!" Tom exclaimed. "We'd be glad to take your money!"

"Wait a minute," Cramp interjected. "Do you really want to help Wendell?"

"Yes. I have said so."

"Alright. Come into the back room. I've got a proposition to put to you."

"I'm all ears," said Joan with a stage leer.

They followed Arthur into the campaign manager's private office and sat down. Joan seemed singularly ill-suited to the hard, utilitarian chair, especially when she crossed her silky, exquisitely elegant legs.

"This is the proposition, Joan," said Cramp. "We have four candidates in the race. We figure we're in second place, a close second, but we need time for Wendell's strength to grow. Are you with me?"

"Yes, Arthur. You express yourself so masterfully."

"Now you're shitting me." Cramp was embarrassed. "If there was another candidate, it could go to four ballots."

"And you want me to be another candidate. To be your stalking horse?"

"Yes," Cramp seemed amazed that Joan had grasped the situation so easily.

"Okay. I'll do it."

"Amazing! That's wonderful! Use some of that twenty thousand to put up your deposit. The rest you'll have to find some roundabout way to get it to us because all contributions have to be made public."

"Consider it done, Arthur," Joan said sexily.

"Okay. Now go out the back door and don't tell anyone you've been here. File your papers right away and put on the best campaign you can. But not too good."

Joan threw back her meticulously coiffured tresses and laughed. "What fun! I'm going to enjoy this. It'll be my greatest role."

"Okay, Joan, off you go before someone sees you."

"Haven't you forgotten something, Arthur?"

"What? Cramp was flustered.

"I presume that when I am knocked off, I should make a big show of taking my supporters over to Wendell. That right?"

"Oh yes. That's it exactly."

"Anything else?"

"Like what?"

"Since I guess we can't meet until the convention, I'll need each of your private numbers."

"Of course," said Tom and scribbled on a piece of paper.

Joan took it, and with a toss of her head, sashayed to the back door and disappeared from view.

"What an extraordinary woman," said Tom in awe. "I think we have all underestimated her."

"She makes me feel like I've been seduced with my pants on." Cramp growled.

Joan was as good as her word. Within four hours, she had filed her papers, and it was all over the news that a Hollywood star would be seeking the party leadership. Later that evening, it became the talk of the province. On talk shows and phone-in programs, all manner of people were welcoming her move with great enthusiasm.

Wendell, who knew nothing about the back room deal, said he warmly welcomed Joan's participation. When asked, Gardiner seemed nonplussed and stuttered about candidates "coming out of the woodwork." Boudreau pretended he could not remember who she was. Angus MacKinnon, in what may have been his first mistake of the campaign, said the race would be much more interesting with a pretty face as one of the contenders.

"I've just had a terrible thought, Tom." Cramp said.

"What's that, Arthur?"

"What if she isn't knocked off on an early ballot, stays in the fight, and beats us?"

"Holy crap!"

Jeremy Akerman

41

When Heidi heard the news about Joan Howard's candidacy for the party leadership, she was excited that a woman was in the race, and more so because Joan had long been her favourite actress. She and her sisters had long been party members for their father's sake, but until now Heidi had not had her interest sufficiently piqued to actively participate. She liked Wendell Proctor a great deal, but she thought Joan was a glamorous "happening" which could mobilize women and put some pizzazz into the campaign.

Somewhat to her surprise, because it was the first time they had ever shown the slightest interest in politics, Poppy and Petra felt the same way.

Heidi knew that Anthony was active in the party, so asked him how they could get involved. He told her that their constituency, Halifax Citadel, would be selecting delegates the following night. He also said they might stand a good chance of being selected as delegates because a number of the party activists would be away in the Chester area, closing their summer cottages for the year.

So it proved. The meeting, which had been called at short notice, was not well attended. Anthony got the largest vote. Heidi was number fifteen and the twins just scraped in at nineteen and twenty. In fact, there was only a small handful of unpopular, obstreperous members who were unsuccessful in becoming delegates.

Armed with their credentials, the three Granger girls went

straight to Joan Howard's campaign headquarters and volunteered their services. The place was already abuzz with activity, and was populated by an extraordinary number of attractive young women, whose ranks they joined. This small army of adherents quickly became known as "Howard's Angels."

~

Earlier in the day two other events occurred, but nobody had the slightest inkling that there was any connection between them.

The first was the delivery of the Chief Medical Examiner's final report, pursuant to the Fatality Investigations Act 2001, into the death of former premier Brenton Granger. The manner of death was determined to have been asphyxiation by drowning. The autopsy had revealed that a significant amount of alcohol had been consumed by the victim, which may have contributed to his lack of control, and could have led to his involuntarily entering the water. The victim's inability to swim was noted as being relevant.

Other than an abrasion to the victim's right shin where he had made contact with the wharf's railings, no injury, either internal or external, had been detected, which led the Examiner to declare that no third party had been involved in the death.

The statement of Reginald Parsons was read into the record, relating the circumstances of the victim's activities prior to the death. Mr. Parsons was not in court because the police had been unable to trace his whereabouts.

The Chief Medical Examiner's official verdict was Death by Misadventure.

At approximately the same time as the Chief Medical Examiner was rendering his verdict on the death of Brenton Granger, a number of city blocks away, Police Chief Walter O'Malley and Inspector Leblanc were reviewing the Examiner's report on the deaths of two persons discovered in Flinn Park. Each had been killed, by person or persons unknown, by a single shot to the head by a Glock 43X, a handgun of which there existed as many as twenty million copies in North America. The victims were determined to have been shot elsewhere and taken to the location at which they were found.

There were no items on the bodies to indicate their identities, and while DNA analysis showed they were likely brother and sister, neither appeared in the National DNA data bank of convicted offenders. Likewise, dental records were unproductive.

O'Malley quizzed his inspector carefully. "No leads?"

"Absolutely none."

"Missing Persons reports?"

"None that would match."

"What's your best guess?"

"If we were in Chicago or Toronto even, I would say it was a mob hit."

"They were that careful, that thorough? That professional?"

"Meticulous in every respect. No third party DNA, no prints, no residual evidence, nothing."

"Okay." O'Malley sighed. "Close the investigation. No Action, pending further developments."

42

The following morning several items from the party office came to Tom's attention. The first was a notice that the deadline for nominations as candidates for the party leadership had closed as of midnight. The next was the list of those who had been officially nominated together with their constituencies, and the colour which had been assigned to each, determined by a blind draw. This latter was thought by the Executive to be necessary so as to distinguish between the various camps at the convention centre.

Boudreau, Albany. Argyle. Yellow.
Gardiner, Mark. Kings South. Green.
Howard, Joan. Shelburne. Red.
MacKinnon, Angus. Antigonish. Orange.
Proctor, Wendell. Halifax Needham. Blue.

Then came a heavy package containing a list of all delegates chosen to date. Well over three-quarters had already been selected, which Tom thought significant, given that the deadline was not until the end of the week.

When he came to the list from Halifax Citadel, he was surprised to see four Grangers listed, and particularly the twins, whom he had been led to believe scarcely had a brain between them.

As his eyes hovered over Heidi's name, the pain of her loss returned with a jolt. He missed her so very much.

Pulling himself together, Tom took the lists and divided them into bundles, and then called those who had been at Wendell's selection meeting, instructing them to come in and get their assignments.

When Arthur Cramp arrived later, he and Tom went through the lists, trying to reassess the strength each candidate might receive on the first ballot. After a period of calculation, Tom called out the names, to which Cramp gave his guess.

"Boudreau."

"A hundred and fifty."

"Gardiner."

"One hundred and twenty."

"Howard."

"Ah," said Cramp. "When we got her into this, I would have said fifty at the most, but now, I'm not so sure."

"Seventy-five?"

"More like a hundred, would be my guess."

"Wow!" Tom exclaimed. "I hope this stunt is not going to backfire on us."

"It might look like that from time to time, but I have complete faith in that woman. I didn't think so before, but I now think she is someone to reckon with."

"Okay, Arthur. If you say so. Moving on. MacKinnon."

"Four hundred."

"Proctor."

"Three hundred and forty."

"That is too tight," said Tom. "If Angus starts with four hundred it means he has three more ballots to accumulate only one hundred and sixty-five votes, whereas Wendell would have to gain two hundred and sixteen."

"It will depend on who has the greater momentum," said Cramp. "If Wendell is rolling along, and MacKinnon is only picking up bupkus, we can do it."

"That assumes, of course, that our calculations are close to reality."

"Yeah. And then there's the rule that if something can go wrong, it will go wrong!"

"Our throwing Joan into the ring could be a huge unknown factor. She'll draw a lot of the younger crowd."

"Don't worry about Joan. I told you," Cramp said emphatically. "I trust her."

"All we can do is keep plugging away and hope for the best," said Tom. "And, Arthur..."

"What?"

"Don't forget to take your lists." He pushed a pile across the table. "I expect you to have contacted all these people by Wednesday, and to report back to me."

"Proper slave driver, aren't you?" Cramp glared at him. "Okay. I'll do my part."

~

That afternoon, Wendell came by to report that he had just come back from Cape Breton, where his reception was much better than he expected. He had had meetings with four constituency associations over the past few days, and was surprised to learn that none of the other candidates had been there before him.

He felt this might give him an advantage, except that he noted there seemed to be a lively organization for Joan Howard. At each of the meetings there had been a clutch of girls and young women waving signs bearing Joan's portrait against a bright red background.

On balance, Wendell felt he might get as many as seventeen delegates from Cape Breton Centre-Whitney Pier, about twelve from each of Sydney-Membertou and Glace Bay-Dominion, and ten from Northside-Westmount.

Of course, Tom knew from bitter experience that the candidate's assessment of his own strength was never wholly reliable, but if Wendell was right, it would be a handsome fifty votes in the bag.

Wendell indicated that he had no idea what, if any, support he had in Victoria, Richmond and Inverness counties because he had made no contacts there. Tom did not say so, but he felt certain that MacKinnon had all the delegates from those areas.

He sent Wendell back out to continue his punishing routine, with every hope it might eventually reap dividends.

43

The weeks raced by. Tom had never worked so hard in his life, often not going home at night but sleeping at the headquarters on a collapsible cot in the back room.

Every call which could have been made, was made, and often twice and three times. Wendell had been on the road continuously. Every one of the original group had kept their word and had done everything possible to win over the people they knew, except Maddingly, who used the excuse of being premier to absent himself.

Social events had also been held, to raise money and morale, and Grace and Cynthia co-hosted several of them. The two hitherto-bitter antagonists had discovered that neither was as bad as she was painted, and their love for Wendell had brought them to a point, if not of endearment, at least of recognition that they had far more in common than what divided them.

Tom had been disappointed, if not actually surprised, to learn from the person assigned to calling the delegates from Halifax Citadel that Anthony was committed to Mark Gardiner, while Heidi and the twins were actively campaigning for Joan. It crossed his mind that this could be an excuse to call her, but he instantly knew it would accomplish nothing positive.

Meanwhile, the weather was getting progressively colder as the day of reckoning approached. Very little which was out of the ordinary had happened. There had been no scandals, no great acts of treachery, and few unexpected developments. On paper, at least, the overall situation remained much as it had weeks previously.

Finally, the eleven hundred or so delegates converged on the Nova Centre and the convention was called to order. As usual Arthur Cramp summed up the general mood.

"Let battle commence," he growled.

On the first night, the candidates addressed the assembled company. It was thought that a debate would be too unruly, not to mention undignified, so each candidate had a maximum of twenty minutes to make their speech, in an order determined by drawing lots. Albany Boudreau drew the first position, Angus MacKinnon the second, Joan third, Wendell fourth and Mark Gardiner last.

Naturally, opinions differed, but the general consensus was that Boudreau had spoiled his opportunity by trying to be a funny man under circumstances which most delegates considered serious. Everyone acknowledged that MacKinnon's speech was powerful, but his natural arrogance occasionally broke through the surface of a polished performance. Gardiner, despite having secured the best spot in the line-up, failed to explain why he was the right man for the job, and seemed to make much of the strange assertion that he was "a man in a hurry."

Wendell delivered a superb effort, well structured, and measured, indicating considerable gravitas. His peroration was particularly good and brought many delegates to their feet. Both Tom and Arthur agreed he could not have done better.

But the star of the night was Joan, who positively glittered and glowed. Her voice rang rich and clear and was punctuated by the numerous "Howard's Angels" (among whom Heidi was prominent) leaping up and cheering wildly. She radiated beauty and her timing was immaculate.

Tom thought it a triumphant *tour de force*, the likes of which he could not remember having heard before. It made him nervous, but he could see that Arthur loved every second of it, even joining in the prolonged applause. He placed a hand on Tom's arm, smiled, nodded and walked away to the bar.

The voting started at ten the next morning.

44

The Executive had chosen as Convention Chairperson Bessie Boone, a much-loved party icon, who had been an MP at Ottawa for almost thirty years. Bessie carried her seventy-five years well, being upright and dignified. She also had an aura of authority, and a strong voice which carried above the chatter and babble. When she gavelled the convention to order at ten o'clock, the place was absolutely packed.

A section of the bleachers had been allotted to each candidate, whose supporters displayed his or her designated colour in one way or another. From left to right, starting at the entrance, the Boudreau supporters wore yellow hats and waved signs of the same hue. Next, the Gardiner people had green sashes and buttons. Joan's section was ablaze, her supporters wearing bright red sweaters and waving huge scarlet banners. MacKinnon's backers carried tall Day-Glo orange signs saying ANGUS, while in Wendell's section, his troops were attired in bright azure blue tee shirts.

As Tom and Arthur surveyed the area, it was apparent that their predictions would not prove to be accurate. It appeared that all but one of the candidates would do less well than they anticipated. The candidate who seemed to be exceeding expectations was Joan.

"How many votes do you think she might get now, Arthur?"

"A hundred and fifty, maybe."

"That many? That concerns me."

"Calm down," said Cramp in a fatherly tone, "everything is going to be alright."

"Arthur, do you know something I don't?"

"Tom, I know a lot of things you don't know," Cramp said with a wink.

The delegates lined up at the voting stations, and when the last of them had voted, the officials and scrutineers retired to count the ballots.

"Care to take any bets, Arthur?" Tom asked.

"I don't think I will. But however it comes out, I predict I will be pleasantly surprised."

"What is that supposed to mean?"

"Shhh. Here she comes with the result."

Bessie Boone appeared on the dais and pulled the microphone towards her. She cleared her throat, put on her reading glasses, and held the paper out in front of her. "I have the results of the first ballot."

There was absolute silence.

"I will read them in the alphabetical order of the candidate's surnames: Boudreau, Albany: 68."

The crowd was subdued, but the severe disappointment among the Boudreau forces was palpable.

"Gardiner, Mark: 101."

There was a collective murmur, but audible groans from the Gardiner troops.

"Howard, Joan: 259."

The convention gasped, and the "Howard's Angels" went wild, whooping, leaping up and down, and hugging each other. Arthur dug Tom in the ribs with his elbow.

"MacKinnon, Angus: 343."

While MacKinnon's forces madly waved their signs, two pipers stood up and played snatches of the Jacobite air *Là Sliabh an t-Sior-raim.*

"Proctor, Wendell: 318."

It was the turn of Wendell's supporters to cheer. It was a good result, although some thirty votes short of Tom's assessment. He glanced at Cramp to see if any disappointment registered on his face, but the old man was grinning broadly.

"This means that Albany Boudreau will drop off," Bessie Boone announced. "We will now proceed to the second ballot. Thank you, Albany, for your participation and dedication to our party."

There was a round of applause for Boudreau, which he accepted with a wave and a smile. The ranks of those around him were now severely depleted.

"If Wendell was thirty short of our projections, at least Angus was sixty behind," Tom said.

An hour later, the results of the second ballot were announced.

"Gardiner, Mark: 75."

He had lost support. He sat looking miserable as his friends patted him on the back. His dream was over and his name was removed from the ballot.

"Howard, Joan: 287."

This was a gain of fewer than thirty votes. She had momentum but it was now slower.

"MacKinnon, Angus: 372."

MacKinnon had gained some votes, but not many. The pipers played *Blue Bonnets over the Border*.

"Proctor, Wendell: 358."

"Yes!" Cramp shouted. Wendell had gained forty votes, indicating that he had the greatest momentum. He was closing in on MacKinnon.

The third ballot took less time to tabulate. Cramp scribbled on a piece of paper and handed it to Tom. Bessie Boone was approaching the microphone so he hurriedly pushed it into his pocket.

"Howard, Joan: 331."

There was a tremendous round of applause to acknowledge Joan's remarkable effort. No-one applauded louder than Arthur Cramp. Some of her "Angels" were crying because this meant she was out of the contest.

"MacKinnon, Angus: 384."

Angus MacKinnon had increased by only twelve votes, not an encouraging sign for him.

"Proctor, Wendell: 382."

There was a huge collective gasp, followed by a babble of conversation as everyone realized the front runners were within two votes of each other.

Arthur Cramp turned to Tom, his eyes glinting. "Now watch and learn," he said.

From the front row of her section, Joan rose and slowly walked around the arena. She gave Angus a little wave as she passed him, and ended up in front of Wendell. She shook his hand and then hugged him.

As she did so, her entire section of supporters took off their red sweaters to reveal that they were wearing Wendell's blue tee shirts underneath.

"You cunning old bastard," said Tom to Cramp with undisguised admiration.

He took the crumpled paper out of his pocket. It said: It said: It said: "Wendell by 280."

The final ballot was almost exactly as Cramp had predicted.

MacKinnon, Angus: 407
Proctor, Wendell: 691

The crowd went crazy and the noise level rose to new heights of cacophony. Signs and banners were being thrown into the air. Somewhere Zandili was leading an impromptu choir, singing, "We shall not be moved".

Hundreds of people were swarming around Wendell, wanting to shake his hand. Towering head and shoulders above the crowd, he smiled, looked up to the gallery where Tom was standing, and gave the thumbs up. Tom grinned and returned the gesture.

"We've got ourselves a new premier," said Cramp. "You should be very pleased with yourself, Tom. You worked like a slave for this moment. I sure hope Wendell doesn't forget it."

45

Wendell Proctor was sworn in as Premier of Nova Scotia by the Lieutenant Governor the day after his election as the leader of his party.

Unless one counted James W. Johnston, a subject of some controversy, Wendell was the first black premier in the province's history. Johnston, who was born in Jamaica in 1792 under supposedly mysterious circumstances, is claimed by some black Nova Scotians as one of their own, but little proof has been adduced to support the assertion. His grandfather came from Scotland and his mother was Elizabeth Lichtenstein, whose father came from Kronstadt, Russia, so the claim seems unlikely.

No such doubts surrounded Wendell Proctor, both of whose parents were undeniably black, as indeed were his grandparents.

On the evening following his swearing in, Wendell's mother, Blossom, and his sister, Grace, organized the biggest party Halifax's North End had ever seen. It took place in about a dozen houses simultaneously, and Wendell moved from one to the other, accepting congratulations and good wishes.

On each visit he was accompanied by his fiancée, who was now accepted by the community with open arms. Grace had rehearsed a little speech in which she said that she had always known that Cynthia was the right girl for her brother. Each time she delivered this monologue, Matthew, Wendell and his father, Douglas, would suppress their smiles and exchange knowing glances.

Wendell's changes to cabinet included Mark Gardiner's demotion to Tourism and Culture. Bill Clark came in as Minister of Transport and Public Works, and Angus MacKinnon moved from Transport to Economic Development. Joan Howard was named Deputy Premier, with responsibilities for the Cabinet Office and Intergovernmental Affairs. Harland MacIvor left the cabinet, but all others remained in the posts they had previously occupied. Zandili was to be the new Speaker, to replace Bill Clark.

Wendell offered Tom his pick of positions, but he asked only for the position of Leader of the House to be combined with that of Chief Whip, a combination the new premier thought made eminent sense.

Wendell told Tom that he was looking at April for his wedding with Cynthia and, confidentially, that he would likely go to the polls shortly thereafter.

The premier hosted a small, exclusive party for his closest associates at an expensive Halifax restaurant, at which Arthur Cramp drank a quantity of single malt whisky and told the story of how he and Joan Howard had put Wendell into office. He acknowledged that they received invaluable assistance from "young Tom."

They ate a splendid meal, laughed a lot, and those who were not inebriated from the liquor were intoxicated by Joan's breathtaking beauty.

Zandili convened the Legislature for a brief session to conduct housekeeping business and pass a few minor pieces of legislation. The new premier was greeted with cheers and desk thumping as he entered the chamber, and accepted the congratulations of the Chair and from the leaders of the opposition parties. He thanked the House and drew attention to the election of the first black person, Wayne Adams, which had occurred in 1993.

Within a few weeks the House adjourned, and the province's focus turned to Christmas.

46

Three months had passed and the city was in the grip of an icy winter. Snow lay, not deeply, but tenaciously on roof tops, gardens, parks, and some sidewalks. A bitter north-westerly wind found its way into every unprotected corner, causing the residents to retreat into layers of clothing, huge mufflers and thick woolly hats.

Tom's office windows were caked with ice and he could barely see the trees outside, where, it seemed like an eternity ago, he had watched Uncle Arthur and Brenton Granger huddled in private conversation.

The Proctor administration had functioned well so far, there having been no major problems or irritants. Knowing his chance had passed, Angus MacKinnon became a strong, positive force in the cabinet. There was little chance of anything getting passed unless both he and Chester MacCormack were agreed on it, and none at all if the Premier and Joan Howard were opposed.

Boudreau and Gardiner had buckled down to their departmental responsibilities, seldom straying into areas beyond their own remits. The backbenchers were content.

The biggest risk taken by Premier Proctor was the appointment of Zandili, because of her fiery temper, but she exceeded expectations and had become a model of moderation and respectability.

But the ache inside Tom had never left him, and was intensified one day when Stephanie came into his office for coffee and a chat. After discussing a variety of matters, she fell silent for a minute.

"I suppose you've heard the news?" she asked.

"News? What news?

"About Heidi Granger."

"What about Heidi?" His heart was in his mouth.

"She got engaged."

"Oh." It came like a poleaxe to the heart. "Who to?"

"Some young guy she met when she was at university, I think."

"That was quick work," said Tom bitterly.

"That's what I was thinking. Does it still hurt?"

"Just as much as ever."

"That's too bad for you," she said, and added: "And for me too."

"I'm sorry, Steph. I wish things had been different. It seems to be a rule of life that we can't choose who we love."

"Isn't that the truth!"

~

About two weeks later, Tom's secretary said there was a call for him from Lucille.

Tom grabbed the phone. "Heidi?"

"Hello. How are you Tom?"

"As well as can be expected."

"You must be glad that Wendell won the leadership. I'm happy for you."

"Thanks. I guess I should be happy for you, too. I hear you got engaged."

"You heard?"

"Stephanie told me a few weeks ago."

"Tom, I have to talk to you." Heidi sounded serious. "Can you get away at one o'clock?"

"I guess I could," Tom answered uncertainly. "What's it about?"

"Meet me at the park bench. You know the one we used to sit

on?"

"How could I forget?"

"See you then."

When Tom reached the park, he saw that Heidi was on the bench, but that she was not alone. A young man was sitting beside her. Tom wondered what anguish he would have to endure as a result of his having agreed to this meeting.

As he got closer, he saw that Heidi had changed. She wore more makeup than she used to, and looked older and more sophistic-ated. The man was a handsome, well-built fellow approximately Heidi's own age.

When they saw him approaching, they stood up.

"Hello, Tom. This is Scott."

"Hello, Scott." Tom tried hard not to be surly.

Scott looked as ill-pleased to see Tom as Tom was to be meeting him.

"Look, Heidi, I've got to go or I'll be late. I'll see you tonight."

When Heidi gave Scott a goodbye kiss, Tom looked away, won-dering why she had to increase his torment. Scott disappeared into the park.

"He seems like a nice man," said Tom, not meaning it.

"He is."

"If he loves you half as much as I did, you've got yourself a bar-gain."

"Let's walk for a bit. Okay?"

The wind was now biting at their necks as they leaned over some railings, watching children play on the small rink.

"What is it you want, Heidi?" Tom was in no mood to play games.

"Do you still feel the same way about me as you used to?"

"For God's sake, Heidi! Why are you doing this? What does it matter now?"

"Please answer me."

"I've been doing everything I can to try to forget you. But if you must know, I think I'll probably love you till the day I die."

"I've just told Scott that if you would have me back, the engagement is off."

Tom gaped at her in disbelief.

"I got thrown off course by a bunch of stuff, mainly Dad's death, and a promise I made to my mother. But I now know what I want, and I don't care about anything else."

Tom continued to stare at her, feelings of joy, confusion and anger wrestling for dominance inside him. "Let's get out of this damn cold!" he finally said, striding away.

They found a small café and, still in their topcoats, sat warming their hands on steaming cups of coffee.

"I'm still absolutely nuts about you, Heidi, but I wouldn't even consider getting back with you unless you agree to certain conditions."

"What are they?"

"No more cloak and dagger, for a start. First thing we do is to see your mother and lay it all out for her. Then we move in together. Then, if we can still stand each other, we get married and have babies."

"I didn't know you could be so masterful," said Heidi, grinning from ear to ear. "How can I resist such an offer? You've got yourself a deal."

"Then we do it tonight. No putting it off."

"Come to the house at eight."

"Just try and stop me."

~

It was dark and freezing when Tom parked his car. Snow was blowing from the power lines. He took a deep breath, then walked up the driveway to the front door.

Heidi had been waiting for him and let him in. "Be warned," she whispered, "Anthony is here."

Tom had never been inside this house. The many meetings he had with Brenton Granger were always in his or the premier's office.

Before he and Heidi could exchange another word, Anthony appeared in the hallway.

"Hello, Anthony. How are you? It's good to see you again."

"You can cut the crap, Aldridge. I know why you're here and I think it's outrageous."

"Anthony," said Heidi, "is this really necessary?"

"I've been against this sordid business from the start. When Heidi dumped you I thought it was the first example of common sense she's shown in years."

"Screw you!" Heidi snapped at him.

"My father must be turning in his grave."

"How dare you!" Heidi was angry. "Come on, Tom. Ignore the spoiled little brat. You didn't come here to see him."

Florence had forsaken her wheelchair some time since, so now occupied a large arm chair by the fire. Anthony moved behind his mother and stood there like a vulture.

Heidi had told her mother that Tom was coming this evening, so she was civil to him, if not exactly warm.

"I suspected Heidi was lying to me when she told me there was nothing going on between you two. She should have come clean to me at the time. I'm a much tougher old broad than my children give me credit for. I confess, Tom, it will take me a while to be comfortable with this arrangement, but Heidi says she loves you and will be happy with you, and happiness is a rare commodity. That fact that she still feels this way after months of your being separated tells me this is the real thing."

At this, Anthony snorted and cleared his throat.

"Oh, be quiet, Anthony. This is none of your business."

She then turned back to Tom. "Shall you marry or live in sin?"

"We will marry" said Heidi very firmly. Then added with a giggle, "After we've lived in sin for a while."

"Well, I won't be going to any wedding!" Anthony said.

"You're over twenty-one, even if you don't act like it," Florence said acidly. "It's your prerogative to exercise. I shall certainly attend the wedding and I shall buy something very expensive to wear for the occasion."

47

The next morning Tom walked over to the Premier's office as if he were waltzing to a full orchestra playing Strauss. He had never in his life been in a better mood, and never felt as positive about the future.

He greeted Mrs. Wilson cheerfully. "I'm here to see the Boss"

"I'm sorry, Mr. Aldridge, but he is tied up all morning."

"He'll see me, Mrs. W."

"He's with the chairman of the Public Utilities Board. I'd have to interrupt them."

"Interrupt away, Mrs. W. Tell him it's about a double wedding."

"Very well, Mr. Aldridge," said Mrs. Wilson, frowning. "A double wedding?"

"That's right."

Shaking her head doubtfully, Mrs. Wilson opened the padded outer door, gently tapped on the inner one, and put her head round the door. "Excuse me, Premier, but I have Mr. Aldridge here who says he must speak to you about a double wedding."

Wendell looked up, at first not comprehending, then thumped the desk, and grinned like a child with a box of candy. "Hot damn! Can you give us the room for a few minutes, please, Ed?"

"Certainly, Premier," said the Board Chairman who slipped out of the side door.

"What the hell?" he demanded of Tom.

"I'm getting married. That is definite. The only question is whether or not it will be a double wedding with you and Cynthia."

"That's wonderful! But who...who is it...not Stephanie?"

"No, no, it's Heidi. We're back on, we're out in the open, and it's full steam ahead. Everything's fine!"

"Good God! I thought that was over. This is a miracle!"

"So how about it?"

Wendell sat back and rubbed his hand over his face, thinking hard. "You're Catholic, and I'm a Baptist. That might present some problems."

"If Reverend Oliver and Father Geoffrey can't work out a joint service for the premier of the province, I should be very surprised."

"I guess you're right, but we might have to have it on neutral territory."

"Well, Neither Cornwallis Street Church nor St. Michael's would be big enough. There would be a huge attendance."

"Say what," said Wendell grinning, "why not have it at the Nova Centre? The scene of our fabulous win?"

"Now, that is a great idea. This will be the event of the year."

Wendell's face clouded over. He frowned and scratched his head. "Maybe not," he said quietly. "Sit down, Tom. I wasn't going to tell you yet, but I may as well get it over with."

"What's up?"

"You're the only one of knows yet, so keep it to yourself. I've decided to see the Lieutenant Governor this week and have him issue the writ for a general election on April 15th."

"Excellent! I assume we've had some polling done."

"Yes, and the polls look good. It's doubtful if we could come back with Granger's majority, but if we're lucky it would be almost as good. Maybe we'd lose as many as six seats."

"Oh. Which ones?"

"It's difficult to say with this kind of poll, but it looks as if Joan, Mark and Bill would be among the losers."

"Joan? That would be a disaster."

"I know, but hers is a very marginal seat. Until she squeaked in at the by-election, it was held by the other crowd for forty years. I'd like to find a new, safe seat for her, but you know the difficulties with trying to impose a candidate from the top."

"She could have my seat," said Tom quickly.

"Are you serious? Could she really?" Wendell was surprised because selflessness was not a common quality in politics.

"Sure. If I could be your Chief of Staff after the election."

"Yes, you know it! Why not? That could work out. Gordon's due for retirement anyway."

"Is it a deal?"

"It's a deal, old friend. Your constituency association won't kick up a fuss?"

"One or two of them might moan, but I'll sic Heidi on them. She'll charm the pants off them."

"Good. I'll tell Joan tonight. "

"Where does this leave the wedding?"

"Let's turn it over to Heidi and Cynthia...and Grace, of course, we can't leave her out of it. Let's have them organize it for late May."

"Sounds wonderful."

~

That evening, Tom and Heidi drove across town.

"Where are we going, Tom?"

"To see my grandmother."

"Your grandmother is dead. I hope we're not going to a cemetery at this time of night."

"No, this is my *Bubbe*. She's an old Jewish lady who kind of adopted me when my first wife was killed. Andrew was just a kid then."

"Why have you never told me about her?"

"She and her daughter were against our being together, so I didn't want to burden you."

"I see. Are they still opposed to us?"

"I'm not sure, but as soon as Chedva meets you she will be on-side. She will love you. Sarah is another kettle of fish. She may need time."

"Will Andrew be there?"

"Yes. He'll be there."

"Oh dear. This could be a real ordeal."

"No, he has completely come around. Now he is one of our big-gest boosters."

Tom's predictions proved correct, except that Sarah was not ac-tually hostile, but rather cool and polite. It took less than twenty minutes before Chedva was hugging Heidi as if she was one of her own. Andrew gave moral support, by having a more than usual amount of Chedva's 21-year-old Caperdonich, and loudly singing Heidi's praises.

By the end of the evening, with help of the whisky, even Sarah was thawing. A little drunk, she sat back on the chesterfield and sighed, "*Alts iz gut vos ends gezunt.*"

~

"What did Sarah say at the end?" Heidi asked when they were back in the car.

"All's well that ends well." Tom said.

"How lovely."

They drove on in silence for a few minutes

"How on earth did you become engaged to Joe College?" Tom asked.

"His name is Scott," she said, punching him in the arm. "I wanted to be married and have kids, and the whole world was telling me I couldn't do it with you."

"Now you can."

"Yes. I can, and I am looking forward to it very much."

She stretched over and kissed his cheek.

48

Apart from the premier, who spoke at rallies all across the province, a special team of Angus MacKinnon, Stephanie and Chester MacCormack, whose own seats were considered to be completely safe, was assigned to a barnstorming tour, carrying the message into every nook and cranny. Tom took a back seat in the campaign, running the premier's engagements and travel arrangements from Halifax, which meant he had some, but not much, time to spend with Heidi.

In any event, Heidi was quite occupied helping to run Joan's campaign in Tom's old constituency. He had been right about her persuasive powers, in that she had no difficulty soothing the dissidents. Those who were not won over by Heidi's tender ministrations, were bowled over by Joan's incandescent appearance and personality. Heidi adored and admired Joan, and was grateful to be her friend and helper.

While the election was in full swing, another very different team was running its campaign. Headed by Grace, to whom Cynthia ceded the leadership, the wedding arrangements proceeded apace. They visited Joan's election headquarters from time to time to consult Heidi, who was more than content to leave the details in their capable hands.

There had been some difficulty with a ceremony of two very different denominations, because, while neither Reverend Oliver nor Father Geoffrey needed little persuading, the latter was required to obtain permission from his bishop. The old prelate was dubious and could find no precedents for what was requested. But his chaplain gently pointed out that if the church refused the premier —and moreover one who was black—the repercussions might be "unhelpful".

The bishop reluctantly agreed and ordered that Father Geoffrey proceed.

Surprisingly, there were few hitches in the campaign, no scandals and only a few unpleasant clashes. The Leader of the Opposition conducted an excellent, clean fight, although the third party leader, attempted unsuccessfully to accuse the government of racism on the grounds that Wendell was a "puppet of the white vested interests."

Election Day dawned bright and clear, although still quite cold. The turnout was higher than normal which, in time-honoured fashion, was held to favour the government or work against it, depending upon who was speaking.

The result surprised no-one. The Proctor government won re-election with thirty-eight seats out of a total of fifty-two. The official opposition garnered eleven and the third party won three. Amazingly, the party's candidate who ran in Joan's old constituency was elected, but again with a very slim majority.

The big upsets were the defeat of Albany Boudreau in Argyle, and Harland MacIvor in Kings West. The backbencher who lost his seat had been expected to do poorly because he was seventy-six, in bad health, and an alcoholic. All other cabinet ministers were re-elected with healthy majorities.

The glorious taste of victory was marred only by an event that did not become known until the next day. Arthur Cramp was dead.

Apparently, he was so overjoyed by the party's win, he went into his cellar to get a bottle of Champagne, tripped and fell down twelve steps onto the flagstone floor. The doctor at the hospital said his death had been instant. He gave this communication to Cramp's deceased sister's daughter, who was his only living relative.

All those who might otherwise have been present were attending the victory party downtown.

49

Never had there been such a wedding in Halifax! Every member of Heidi, Cynthia, Wendell and Tom's extended families were there. Every member of the legislature, together with their spouses and partners, were in attendance. All of Nova Scotia's Members of Parliament and senators were there with their spouses. In addition, every party official, both provincial and local, had been invited.

With Cynthia's help, Grace had done a magnificent job in organizing such a gargantuan affair, complete with an orchestra from Symphony Nova Scotia, and a choir of Cornwallis Street Church ladies, in which Grace herself sang like a big-bosomed thrush.

Cynthia, who had originally asked Arthur Cramp to give her away, now had her ancient uncle Simon perform the honour, which he did supported by two crutches. Florence had threatened Anthony with dire consequences unless he relented in his opposition to the wedding, so he finally, reluctantly, gave in and agreed to attend.

Wendell's best man was Matthew, looking immensely proud and spruce, while Blaine had flown in from New York to stand for Tom.

Cynthia wore a shimmering white gown with an abundance of frills, while Heidi chose a simpler dress in very pale blue. It was the unanimous opinion that both brides looked exquisitely beautiful and supremely elegant.

In contrast, Wendell and Tom appeared a little uncomfortable in their tuxedos, occasionally running their fingers inside their collars.

Reverend Oliver and Father Geoffrey had worked out a hybrid form and order of service, which took considerable time and attention, but finally reached a mutually-satisfactory result. They alternated in addressing remarks to the congregation, the Reverend actually performing Wendell's and Cynthia's marriage, and the good father conducting Heidi's and Tom's.

Following the service, the more than four hundred celebrants retired to an adjoining area where Grace had arranged a massive feast of lobster cocktail, rare roast beef, and southern banana pudding. The meal was accompanied by Nova-Scotia-grown Chardonnay and Pinot Noir and, of course, a great deal of Champagne.

The orchestra played Bach's *Sheep May Safely Graze*, Pachelbel's *Canon*, Handel's *Arrival of The Queen of Sheba*, and Grieg's *Wedding at Troldhaugen*, while the choir sang *Here's My Heart, Take My Hand*, *Amazing Grace* and *How Great Thou Art*.

After several hours, Tom and Heidi slipped away to the airport, and went to Bermuda for a week's honeymoon. No such indulgence was afforded to the premier, who was faced with a strike by the Teachers' Union, so his and Cynthia's honeymoon had to be indefinitely postponed.

Florence, whose splendid attire was only overshadowed by that of the brides and Grace, found herself sipping Champagne in a quiet corner with Joan Howard and her husband, Harold.

"All in all," said Joan, "it seems like the past twelve months have been tumultuous for all of us."

"You can say that again," Florence agreed.

Jeremy Akerman

Epilogue

On Cape Breton Island, just past St. Peter's and beyond the canal which links the Bras D'Or lakes with the ocean, is a secondary road which winds its way in a circular route through L'Ardoise, along the coast through Point Michaud to Grand River, and eventually to join the main highway at Soldier's Cove. This is not a busy road and even in summer most tourists miss this quite scenic drive.

Before reaching L'Ardoise, the traveller comes to the small community of Rockdale which boasts a population of just over a thousand souls.

One morning, some months after Premier Proctor's much-publicized wedding, a small, ordinary-looking man went into the general store and asked for cigarettes. The woman behind the counter served him and, as she took his money, squinted at him.

"Don't I know you?" she asked. "Aren't you Billy Bugbee from up yonder?"

"That's me," the man admitted.

"You've been gone a long time. Where have you been? What have you been doing?"

"Oh, this and that. You know, here and there. But I'm back now."

"I guess you'll be taking over your Uncle Walter's place now he's dead."

"That's right," said the man. "Well, I better get going. Thanks."

He left the store, got into his truck, drove up a long dirt road, and pulled into the neglected yard of a weather-beaten old house at the edge of the woods. He had a little luggage, which he took into the house.

Going upstairs, he looked in all the bedrooms, decided which one he would take, and dumped his bags on the bed. He put his few shirts in one drawer and his socks and underwear in another.

He pulled a chair over, climbed on to it and examined the top of the tall wardrobe. Finding it to his satisfaction, he reached into his hold-all and took out a plastic bag. He quickly looked inside before placing the bag on the wardrobe.

The Glock 43X gleamed through its light film of oil.

The end

Jeremy Akerman

About the author

Jeremy Akerman is an adoptive Nova Scotian who has lived in the province since 1964. In that time he has been an archaeologist, a radio announcer, a politician, a senior civil servant, a newspaper editor and a film actor.

He is painter of landscapes and portraits, a singer of Irish folk songs, a lover of wine, and a devotee of history, especially of the British Labour Party.

Printed in the USA
CPSIA information can be obtained
at www.ICGtesting.com
LVHW011401181223
766731LV00005B/228